THE WALL OF RECORDS

WRAK-AYYA: THE AGE OF SHADOWS BOOK EIGHT

LEIGH ROBERTS

DRAGON WINGS PRESS

CONTENTS

Editing by Joy Sephton http://www.justemagine.biz
Cover design by Cherie Fox http://www.cheriefox.com

Sexual activities or events in this book are intended for adults.

ISBN: 978-1-951528-18-8 (ebook)
ISBN: 978-1-951528-21-8 (paperback)

For those who love so deeply, that it surpasses the understanding of mere mortals. And for those who continue to dream and cannot silence their hearts, who from their depths are bound in pursuit of the answer to—

What If?

CHAPTER 1

Tehya screamed. Khon'Tor's eyes flew open. He immediately sat up and took her gently by the shoulders. She flailed against him, scratching his face.

"Tehya, wake up. *Wake up*. You are just having a bad dream; I am here. You are safe." He dodged her flying fingernails.

She looked wildly at him, trying to claw her way up out of a deep sleep. Finally, recognition filled her eyes, and she collapsed against him, sobbing. He pulled her to his chest and rocked her, smoothing the back of her hair.

"I was in the cave with Akar. He was, he was—" her voice broke.

"Sssh, it is alright. You are in our quarters. I am right here with you, and so is Kweeuu. We are not going to let anything happen to you."

She stiffened. "Where is Arismae? Is she here? Is she safe?"

"She is right there where she belongs," he said. *Though how she is still sleeping, I have no idea.* "She is in her nest. Look at me, Tehya. *Look at me.*"

The sternness in his voice helped her return to the present.

"Adoeete. It was horrible. I was back in the cave with Akar'Tor. Only, Arismae had been born. And he had her—and—and—"

"Akar is nowhere near us. He cannot get to you or Arismae. You are safe." Khon'Tor kept talking to her, soothing her. "We have doubled the watchers and guards. There is no way he can get into Kthama."

The nightmares are coming more often. It seems that these bad dreams should have stopped by now. Nothing I do relieves them, not the extra guards, not even the fact that I hardly leave her side. She is losing too much sleep. Surely there is some way to help her through this. Perhaps there is something Adia or Urilla Wuti can do.

Tehya let out a deep breath and melted into Khon'Tor's chest, her fingers buried and intertwined in his thick chest hair.

She had never asked what happened to Akar. Khon'Tor did not want to tell her that they had not found him, that when Haan's Healer went back to help him, he had disappeared. Since she did not ask, he did not bring it up, not wanting to lie to her but not wanting to add to her panic. *If I ever find him, this time I will not hesitate to end him. And I will drag his dead body back to prove that he can no longer bother her or anyone else again.*

Khon'Tor continued to hold his mate and stroked the back of her hair with one hand. Her breathing finally settled, letting him know she was asleep for now. He curled his arms and legs around her like a cage, hoping that she would feel him surrounding her and know she was safe.

When morning came, he watched her slow and measured breathing for a while. He made sure the guards were in place before seeking out Adia.

"What is the matter, Khon'Tor, you looked concerned," the Healer remarked. She was sitting alone at her usual table in the Great Chamber.

"Tehya is still having nightmares about Akar, about when he held her captive. She is not getting enough sleep."

"Sit down," and Adia gestured to the empty place across from her.

"No, I cannot stay; I need to get back to Tehya. Do you have anything that might help her? Short of my producing Akar's dead body?" he asked.

"She does not know he was never found, does she?"

"No, and I have not told her for fear of making things worse. But I imagine she suspects. Perhaps that is what is creating her fears."

"His wounds were severe, and wherever he dragged himself to could not have been far. Or, possibly, he did not survive, and his body was eaten by predators. Tehya said his wounds were infected.

"If I thought Haan would understand, I would hunt Akar'Tor down, but Haan raised him as his own, and there is too much riding on our relationship. I do not have a solution at the moment, but I will allow nothing to put Tehya at risk."

Adia felt the great weight that Khon'Tor was carrying. He still had not told the community every detail and had only recently introduced Arismae, when she was already a week old. For the most part, people had respected their privacy, but they were also wondering about the rest of the story. Akar'Tor's presence at Kthama had been noticeable, and his taking Tehya prisoner had caused enormous stress and turmoil among the community. There did not seem to be anyone at Kthama who did not love Tehya; she had won their hearts, as she had won Khon'Tor's.

"What else did Haan tell Acaraho?"

"His community is split on whether to help us or not. There is a faction that is brewing dissension. Some fear the retribution of the Ancients if the Rah-Hora is broken, and some do not want to help because they do not want the Sarnonn culture to change. It sounds as if he has his hands full with civil unrest. In the meantime, they are moving forward with their preparations—though we still have no idea what those entail."

"What about Hakani's offspring—by Haan?"

"Haan has someone taking care of her. He said she is looking more like us as she grows. I think he is worried about where she will fit in. One of Hakani's friends stepped up to help him with her, and for now, that arrangement is satisfactory."

I would never have thought of Hakani having a friend, thought Adia to herself. *Somewhere between when she left Kthama and when she returned, she must have carved out some type of existence for herself. Though we were never on good terms, I feel bad that she ended her life as she did. The sense of guilt and hopelessness coming off her at the end was unbearable.*

"I will be glad to visit Tehya and take her some Valerian Root. It should help with her anxieties," offered Adia. "But perhaps the best healer will be time. Has she told you at all about what really happened with Akar? Perhaps it would do her good to talk about it."

"She has not said that much. I think she is trying to protect me from knowing just how frightened she was. What she has told me was bad enough. You may be right, Adia. Perhaps talking about it would help her, though she may prefer to share it with someone other than myself."

"It sounds as if it is time for a visit from some fellow females."

Khon'Tor nodded and went in search of First Guard Awan.

Haan sat with Haaka and Kalli, watching his daughter stack and unstack a set of stones and pinecones. Haaka kept a good eye on her, making sure Kalli did not try to eat any of the toys. Haan remembered Hakani saying that Haaka favored him. *Perhaps after Kthama Minor is opened, if we survive it —if any of us survive it— Kalli needs a mother, and Haaka honestly seems to care about her. She does not seem to mind that Kalli is a mixture of Sassen and Akassa; maybe Haaka realizes she is looking into the eyes of our future, at least, the future of those who choose to accept help from the Akassa.*

For days after the young male's disappearance, Haan had organized sentries to go out searching for Akar. If alive, wherever he was, he was well hidden. *Based on how bad Hakani said his wounds were, I do not know that he could survive without help—nor could he have gone far. But they did not find his body either.* Haan did not know what to think.

But time was running out; they needed to begin the preparation ritual, and Haan could not have the problem of Akar'Tor distracting him. Once they joined, all who were engaged in the preparation ritual would no longer function as separate minds.

More powerful when united, they would be focused on their one purpose.

The Leader sighed. *I will have to leave out some of the males to look after Kalli and Haaka. I am not sure we can spare the numbers, but I have no choice. It will have to be enough. If only I had another place for them to go—"*

Kthama. Why did I not think of this sooner? There is no reason she could not go to Kthama. I know Khon'Tor would take her in. She need only stay until this has passed. I must send a messenger to Kthama after I speak with Haaka.

Haaka sat unmoving, looking at Haan while he spoke. When he was done explaining, she pursed her lips before speaking.

She sighed, "If that is what you wish, and it will help relieve your mind, Haan, of course, I will go. I am as curious about them as anyone would be, though also a little nervous. We share a common root. And did you not say they are having the same problems we are—there are not enough of their kind to keep the bloodlines separate?"

"Yes. But the Akassa community is larger and spread across the land, whereas our community has been isolated within itself. I believe that working together, we can solve this problem, though time is not in our favor, and the split in our people is a loss. Those of us who stay here and do not move forward are doomed to weaken and die earlier with each generation."

"Those who stay here? Are we leaving Kayerm?" she asked, concerned.

Haan remembered that he'd had this conversation with Hakani, not Haaka. At Haaka's concern, he wondered if it had added to Hakani's sense of despair and hopelessness.

"It has been pointed out that since there are fewer of us than of those who oppose helping the Akassa, we should be the ones to leave."

"I see," she said quietly. She did not ask where and Haan did not volunteer that as of yet, he had no idea where they would go.

"If you agree to stay at Kthama until we have opened Kthama Minor and the worst is passed, I will send a messenger to their Adik'Tar, Khon'Tor, and ask if he is agreeable to it."

"If that is what you want. I hope they will welcome me," Haaka said.

"They are different from us, Haaka, but that does not mean they are bad. They worship the same Great Spirit and have the same laws as we do. There are many there who will make you feel welcome."

Haaka nodded, turning her attention back to Kalli, who was diligently trying to stuff one of the pinecones into her ear.

Haan rose and left to send a messenger to Kthama.

Yar made the journey to Kthama once again. The last bit of snow was on the ground, and within a few months, the new shoots of spring would peek up through the ground. He had gotten accustomed to going now, and it did not frighten him as it had at first. He had learned that the Akassa were peaceful, and the good news was that by contacting them, he was not breaking the Rah-hora—the bad news was that it had already been broken when Hakani brought Haan and Akar'Tor to Kthama.

Acaraho was meeting with his charges when Yar arrived. They turned as the Great Entrance darkened with Yar's outline blocking out a portion of the morning sun's rays. Acaraho signaled to the males to stand down and went over to speak with the giant Sarnonn.

"Yar, welcome," Acaraho signed.

"Haan needs help from you, Adik'Tar. His daughter and her keeper female need to stay here at Kthama, where they will be safe."

"When, Yar? Now?" asked Acaraho, peering around the giant, half expecting to see them standing behind him.

"No. But shortly. We must soon start the ritual to open Kthama Minor. Haan is only asking if they can stay here until it is over."

Acaraho signed for one of the watchers to find Khon'Tor. With Tehya's state, he was not about to approve one of Haan's people coming to Kthama without Khon'Tor's permission.

Akule gingerly approached the Leader's Quarters. It had almost become a joke now that he was so often selected to bring Khon'Tor his messages. He asked permission to enter because the stone door was open, only the wooden door blocking the entrance.

"Come in, Akule," answered Khon'Tor.

Akule stepped into the Leader's Quarters. It was the first time he had been inside. "What have you come to tell me?" asked Khon'Tor from his place next to Tehya at the eating table. Khon'Tor had become more tolerant of others in his quarters during the many years since he had been paired with a shrew, though he did prefer the old ways when no one else had ever entered—or hardly even thought to approach.

"Acaraho sent me, Adik'Tar. A messenger from Haan has come to ask if one of their females may stay at Kthama for a while with Haan's offspring."

Khon'Tor looked at Tehya, but her features remained calm and relaxed.

"Did he say when, or why, and for how long?"

"Soon, Adik'Tar, and just until Kthama Minor is opened. It has something to do with their preparation ritual."

Acaraho said their community was split—perhaps Haan needs someplace safe for her during the unrest.

He looked back over at his mate. "Did you hear that, Tehya?"

"Yes, Khon'Tor. I have no problem with it. I doubt

that a little offspring and whoever is taking care of her would be a problem."

Khon'Tor thought for a moment. *Who is this female, though? Does she have an allegiance to Hakani? Is this more trouble I could be bringing in? Tehya seems to be fine with it—but my priority is her and our people here. I would not want to deny Haan, but I need more information.*

"Will you be alright here? I need to speak for myself with Haan's messenger."

"Yes, Adoeete, I will be fine. I have Kweeuu and Arismae to comfort me, and it seems that my fears only come at night time."

Khon'Tor leaned over and kissed the top of her head before getting up.

As he stepped through the open doorway, he said to Akule, "Stay outside here with the guards until I return."

Khon'Tor made his way to the Great Entrance and walked up to Yar.

"Greetings, Yar; I need to speak with Haan about this matter."

"Haan is busy, Adik'Tar."

"I am busy too, so take me to him." Khon'Tor took no offense at Yar's abruptness, and he had learned that a direct approach in return worked better with Yar than nuances.

Yah turned and started to leave. Khon'Tor looked at Acaraho, "I guess that means now."

Acaraho said, "I will come with you."

"No. I do not know if Yar means to take me directly to Kayerm or not. We also do not know at what level the dissent is, and we cannot risk both of us," replied Khon'Tor.

"Then at least take others with you," and Acaraho gestured back to his collection of guards.

"You have seen them, Acaraho. I appreciate your concern, but no number of unarmed escorts is going to protect me against half the Sarnonn, and an armed escort would send the wrong message."

Acaraho sighed. "You are right, but I do not like it."

"Two of your males can come, but only to bring word should something happen. I will go no farther than the meadow."

Acaraho signaled, and two of the guards followed Khon'Tor.

Yar led them down the familiar path to the Great River, along her banks, through the thick forest that seemed to stretch on forever, and finally into the valley. At the end of the clearing was the place where Haan had told them to leave messages on the locust trees. Yar signaled for Khon'Tor and his guards to wait there.

"Yar, how far is Kayerm?"

"I cannot tell you."

Khon'Tor sighed. "Ask Haan to bring the female with him."

Yar nodded and continued.

Before too long, Haan and a Sarnonn female

appeared. The female clutched a little offspring to her chest.

Kayerm must be closer than we realized, thought Khon'Tor. *Or else they were already waiting. But it seems unlikely; the female is carrying what can only be Hakani's offspring.*

Haan and Khon'Tor exchanged the Sarnonn greeting, one palm passing over the other. "This is Haaka. She cares for Kalli. She was a friend of Hakani and is part of my pod," said Haan.

Haaka looked at Khon'Tor, her face blank. She was trying to hide her disbelief that she was meeting another Akassa, one who was the spitting image of Akar'Tor and had to be Akar'Tor's father. And worse, one of those whom the Rah-hora had warned they must never contact.

"Adik'Tar, I am happy to meet you," she said.

Khon'Tor looked her in the eyes, unwavering, searching for even a hint of animosity.

"You look at me, Adik'Tar 'Tor. You wonder if a friend of Hakani could be anything but an enemy of yours," Haaka said, steadily returning his gaze.

Khon'Tor raised his eyebrows. *Well, she certainly cut to the chase.* "Yes. *Does it*?" He was also comfortable being blunt.

"Hakani was troubled. The first years she spent with us were a great struggle. Then she seemed to find peace and forgot it all for a time. But when she went to Kthama with Haan, all her pain returned. She could not find peace anywhere anymore. I hope she has found peace now. I mean no harm to you or any of the Akassa."

Khon'Tor continued to stare into her eyes. *I believe her.* He turned to Haan, "When do you want her to come?"

"Haaka will go with you now," said Haan, placing his hand on the small of Haaka's back.

"What?" asked Haaka, her head flipping around to face him. "Now? Leave you now?" Her voice cracked.

"Yes, Haaka, it will not be any easier later. You will be safe there; I would not risk you or Kalli."

Haaka's eyes were wide with alarm.

Khon'Tor glanced down at the offspring Haaka cradled and said to Haan, "She and your daughter will be safe with us." He beckoned Haaka to follow him.

As they were leaving, Khon'Tor asked, "Any news about Akar?"

Haan shook his head. "I will send a messenger if there is and if I am able."

Khon'Tor knew the Sarnonn Leader was referring to whatever preparation ritual had to take place before they could open Kthama Minor. A chill went up his spine, a chill reminiscent of the one he had felt years ago when he first sat listening to the High Council discuss the Waschini and the Wrak-Ayya.

He waved his hand for one of the guards, able to travel faster alone, to go ahead and let Acaraho know that he was returning with the Sarnonn female and

Haan's offspring. He hoped that by the time they arrived, Adia and Nadiwani would also be waiting.

With Yar standing stalwart at his side, Haan silently watched as they walked away.

Eyes straight ahead, Haaka slowed her steps to keep pace with the Akassa Leader. She was not ready to leave Kayerm. That morning, she'd had no idea that she would be going to live with them. Tears welled in her eyes, and she walked with her head down, hoping he would not notice.

When they arrived at Kthama, her eyes grew wide as they followed the walls of the entrance up, up, up to the vast expanse of ceiling dotted with stalactites, then across the room to the tunnels leading off from it. It was far larger than any part of Kayerm. There were several Akassa assembled, perhaps to greet her? Two of them were female, and they approached her with welcoming smiles.

Adia and Nadiwani introduced themselves to Haaka using the combination of Handspeak and the People's verbal language that had proven successful in communicating with Haan.

They both looked at Kalli kindly, surprised despite themselves at how much she had grown.

"Are you hungry? Are you tired?" asked Nadiwani.

"Yes, thank you, I am both tired and hungry," Haaka answered.

Adia stalled, knowing Acaraho was busy having a place prepared for the Sarnonn and Kalli. Some of the females were straightening up one of the spare living areas and working quickly to add a nest and supplies for offspring care.

"Come, I will show you the eating area and get you something to eat. By then, your room should be ready. Is there anything you need that you did not bring? We have basic supplies for you, but if there is something specific, perhaps we can get it for you on the way there," said Adia. "Is your offling eating well? Is everything alright?"

Haaka blushed, "She is not my offling. She is— was—is—Haan's," she stammered. "I left on short notice; I will let you know if I think of anything I need, thank you."

Haaka's eyes continued to dart around as they walked. The room was mostly empty, but those who were there looked up as she and Adia passed by. There had been little time for Acaraho to get word out that a Sarnonn was coming to stay for a while, and their eyes were taking in Haaka and the offspring she carried. Haan had been their first intro- duction to a living breathing Sarnonn, and by comparison, Haaka was much smaller and not as threatening. However, despite all the reassurances that the Sarnonn were peaceful, those who had witnessed it had not forgotten the altercation between Haan and their Leaders shortly after he, Hakani, and Akar'Tor first arrived.

"Sit here, let me get you something to eat," and Adia motioned to one of the rock benches. The Healer walked over to the food preparation area and came back carrying various foodstuffs.

"I do not know what you like, so I brought a variety," she explained after spreading the assortment in front of Haaka.

Haaka's eyes hungrily inspected the wide variety and generous servings. "Thank you."

"How about your—how about Kalli? What have you been feeding her?"

"Mostly mashed fruit and some chewed meat," replied Haaka. This time Nadiwani went to the preparation area and waited there while the females put something together for the little one.

"You can come here anytime you are hungry, Haaka. You do not have to stay in your room; you are not a prisoner here. Please feel free to move about, but I suggest you stay on the upper level until you know your way around. Everything you need is here, and it is easy to get lost at Kthama at first, as all the corridors look the same. There are markers, but I do not know if you would be able to interpret them."

Nadiwani returned with the mashed food for

Kalli. Haaka sat her up and took some of the mash on her fingers to put it into Kalli's mouth. The little offspring readily took it and smacked her little lips. Haaka smiled and hugged her.

As Kalli had finished eating, Acaraho came over, and Adia introduced them.

The High Protector nodded in welcome, "Your quarters are ready if you would like to see them."

Adia helped Haaka wrap up what remained of her meal and Kalli's mash, and carried them for her.

Acaraho led them down the tunnel to Haaka's temporary quarters. He had picked a vacant room not too far down from the Great Chamber, to make it easier on Haaka to find her way around. He motioned for her to enter and stepped aside.

Haaka slowly stepped into the room and stopped. Her eyes scanned the area, running over the separate place for food preparation and finding the sleeping space at the back. It was far more expansive than any of the living areas at Kayerm, even Haan's. Light was coming through some sort of opening in the ceiling.

"We had to improvise on your sleeping area," said Acaraho. He had arranged for many mats to be organized next to each other in several layers to accommodate Haaka's larger size and weight.

"This is lovely, thank you." Kalli started fussing, and Haaka looked around for a place to set her down.

"Here," Adia motioned to where the nest had been prepared.

"I will leave you to help her get settled," and Acaraho nodded to Haaka before leaving the females.

After Haaka had Kalli settled in the little enclosure, Adia pointed to the baskets hanging overhead. "This is your water supply. We usually replace it daily ourselves, but you are our guest, so I will arrange for someone to take care of that for you. The refuse and wastewater go in this one here," she pointed to another on the floor. "Would you like to rest awhile, Haaka? We can fetch you for the evening meal?"

Haaka nodded, glancing longingly at the plush sleeping mats.

After Adia and Nadiwani had left, and having checked on Kalli, Haaka stretched out on the soft space, her body sinking into the generous depth. *No wonder Hakani missed Kthama. I had no idea. There is no comparison. Life at Kayerm must have been challenging after living here. Just the sense of order and cooperation alone is comforting. It will be hard to go back to Kayerm after this. Ah, but then we do not know where we will be going. Haan never said, only that he thought our group would be the one leaving.* Haaka rolled over. *I hope I remember where I am when I wake up. And I hope this is not a dream.*

With Haaka settled, Adia and Nadiwani went to find Urilla Wuti. They were concerned about the passage of time. They needed to begin their preparations for the opening of Kthama Minor. Lifrin had been clear that they should start no later than the new moon.

They had prepared everything that Lifrin had said should be in their diet. The females in the food storage area helped them select what they needed. What they did not have, the females sent some younger offspring out to gather. It was all arranged and stored in the Healer's Quarters.

Other than eliminating meat, most of it was what they usually ate—though in different amounts. The only peculiar addition was to squeeze the juice from apples and let it sit and ferment. They quickly learned that the longer it sat, the more bitter it became. They were also to increase their water intake considerably and burn sage in the quarters every evening before they retired.

The other aspects of preparation involved work on constricting the flow of the Connection. Urilla Wuti assumed this was similar to exercising a muscle —they had to strengthen their boundaries, and the Connection provided their best opportunity to practice.

Nadiwani could not create a Connection. In this case, Urilla Wuti and Adia both felt it was to her benefit. Not being as sensitive to the seventh sense, she would surely not be as impacted by events as they would.

They practiced every morning. First, Urilla Wuti would open the Connection with Adia, and Adia would try to close it against Urilla Wuti's will. Then they would switch and do the same again. After a few hours, they were both exhausted. But it was working, and they found their control was steadily increasing. Nadiwani also worked on trying to control the flow, but so far, she was unable to affect it.

Acaraho gave his mate her privacy during this time, but he was more concerned than he let on. The Healers seemed to think the full moon would signal the time for Haan and his people to open Kthama Minor, so each night, he went out to look for it, counting each day as it grew rounder and fuller.

Awan walked up to Khon'Tor, who was sitting alone in the common area. No one else was within earshot as he said, "It is finished, Adik'Tar."

"I want to see it."

"Considering the secrecy of your request, I know better than to bring it here. It is in the Great Entrance, near where the others are stored."

"Thank you, Awan. I know that was no easy task I asked of you."

"It is an honor to help. Are you sure you will not let me join you on this quest?"

"No. This is something I must do alone."

"Whenever you are ready—"

"Now is fine," and Khon'Tor rose, leaving his unfinished morning meal on the table.

The Great Entrance was empty except for one guard, and Khon'Tor motioned for him to leave so they would be alone.

Awan stepped into a corner and pulled forward a long bundle of considerable weight. He carefully undid the heavy skin wrap and handed to Khon'Tor what was inside.

Khon'Tor examined it, hefting it with his left hand. "It has good balance."

It was a tall, single piece of seasoned locust. Thick in diameter, the bark had been removed, providing a smooth gripping surface. Rows of razor-sharp obsidian points were embedded along both edges of the shaft ending just before a large, sharp spearhead that had been secured to the end.

"That point is also of the hardest obsidian we could find, and it has been finished to your specifi-cations."

Khon'Tor stepped back and swung the weapon around, feeling it slide through the air as easily as it would slice through any opponent—even one his size. He twirled with it, maneuvering with deadly skill.

"Thank you. It is well made."

"I will not ask its purpose, though I have an idea—"

Khon'Tor laid his hand on Awan's shoulder, the People's sign of brotherhood.

"I need a place to store it until I am ready. I cannot keep it in my quarters."

"If you wish, I can keep it in mine. I am alone, with no mate or offspring to come across it. You may enter at any time you need."

Khon'Tor nodded. He did not yet know when he would come for it, but it soothed him to know he would be prepared when the time came.

CHAPTER 2

Khon'Tor returned to their quarters to check on Tehya. He walked in to find an array of dried flowers, branches, and decorative baskets scattered around.

"You were busy while I was away," he said, smiling at his tiny mate.

"Some of my friends brought me all this; they thought I might want to decorate. Do you like it?"

"It is very nice, Saraste'. I had not realized how barren it was in here." Khon'Tor did not say that what made him the happiest, though, was that she had used the word *friends*. *I removed nearly everything before Hakani died—the first time—to prevent her using any of it as a weapon while I slept. But even before that, it was stark. The Leader's Quarters do not look very authoritarian with all these frilly items around, but then this is her home, too. If it makes her happy, then I am happy.*

"Do not worry; when Arismae starts crawling, I

will move the things from the floor to higher places," she added.

"It is very comforting Tehya, and beautiful," he said. "Are we eating in the Great Chamber tonight? Or would you prefer I have something brought here?"

"I would like to join the others if Arismae will cooperate," she smiled, looking down at the tiny bundle in her arms.

"Remember that Haan asked for his offspring to stay here while they prepare to open Kthama Minor? I met with him earlier and brought back the offspring and the female, Haaka, who is caring for her. They are here at Kthama, Tehya. I wanted you to know before you see them."

"Thank you for telling me. I am not worried about the Sarnonn, but I am curious to see the little one, though. Have you seen her?"

"No. Well, I have seen her, but not looked at her closely. I am sure Haaka will not mind showing her to you."

"I wonder how Haaka feels here among us. Alone, no doubt. I know I would. If it had not been for your kindness when I became your mate, leaving my family and everything I knew, I would have probably cried myself to sleep every night for a long time."

"You did cry the first night. I will never forget waking up and finding you in the corner, weeping."

"I did not feel worthy of being the mate of a Leader, let alone one as renowned as yourself."

"You are more than worthy; it is I who am not worthy of you," and he moved over to join her on the sleeping mat.

Tehya tenderly placed her hand on the side of his face.

"I would like to see Oh'Dar. I hope he is at the evening meal," she said.

"I will make sure he is there, and I will come back and get you. And I think you should invite the others back to see how you arranged everything. It is very —pretty."

Kalli's crying woke Haaka from her rest. She cleaned up the offling and laid her back down in the cozy area that the Akassa had prepared.

If I never even left this room, life here would be better than at Kayerm—or anywhere else, I imagine. Oh, Hakani, my friend. I understand why you struggled so. Not only that we were so different from you in appearance and size, I already see the daily toil involved in life at Kayerm compared to when you were living like this. I wonder if all the Akassa communities are this organized?

Before long, she heard someone announce themselves. She opened the stone door to see Nadiwani standing there.

"I have come to bring you to the evening mealtime. Would you like to bring Kalli, or should I send someone to watch her so you can join us alone?"

"I will bring her if you do not mind. I am not yet comfortable leaving her alone, though I mean no offense."

"That is perfectly understandable. I will wait."

Haaka went to collect Kalli and turned to see Nadiwani holding up a circle of some kind of material.

"Here, I made this when I had a young one to watch. I modified it to make it work for you—I hope! Let me help you. It will cradle her against you safely, and free you up a bit."

Haaka had to bend down to let Nadiwani put the lengthened sling over her head. Nadiwani then positioned it against Haaka's body and asked for Kalli and placed her in it.

"This is a very clever idea," Haaka said, looking down at Kalli, who was comfortably suspended and grinning up at her.

"Come on. It is not far."

When she entered the meal area, Haaka could see that those already there were trying not to stare. Nadiwani led her to the counter area and showed her how she could pick out for herself what she wanted to eat. She then introduced Haaka to Mapiya and some of the older females who toiled daily to provide this service.

Everything I am seeing is a better way of doing things. We have lived at Kayerm as long as they have lived at Kthama—yet their ways are far more efficient, structured—what is the word—cooperative? They are focused on helping each other, not letting each pod struggle to do everything on its own.

Whichever of us survives this, however many, I wish that those of us following Haan could all see this way of living, and perhaps, as we move forward, we could copy their ways.

Adia and the others were seated by the time Nadiwani brought Haaka and Kalli over. Unsure of herself, Haaka lowered her eyes as they approached. Nadiwani suggested she sit toward the end of the table so she could see everyone and would have more room. Haaka looked across all the faces, coming to Oh'Dar last. "Oh," she exclaimed before she could catch herself.

Oh'Dar laughed good-naturedly. "I am Oh'Dar, and I am Waschini. My mother, Adia, the Healer, found me when I was just an offspring and rescued me. I have lived here all my life. I know I do not look like them, but I am still one of the People."

"I apologize," signed Haaka, color in her cheeks.

"I am sure I look very fragile and pale to you, Haaka. And are we saying your name properly?"

"Yes. Close enough," Haaka chuckled to herself and smiled.

About then, Khon'Tor and Tehya arrived,

choosing to join Adia's table instead of taking their own more sequestered one.

Tehya went right up to Haaka and greeted her. "I am Tehya; I am the mate of Khon'Tor. May I see your offspring? I have one too!" she said in her cheerful way.

Haaka tried not to stare. *This one looks different from the other Akassa. I wonder if she knows and feels odd about it?* "This is Kalli. She is half Akassa," she said. Tehya peered at the little one in Haaka's sling. With beautiful dark eyes, Kalli looked up at Tehya and grinned.

"She is precious. This is Arismae," and Tehya introduced her offspring.

"I see you have the same kind of sling as Nadiwani brought me. It is a great idea. You have many good ideas here. Better ideas. I can see why Hakani —" Haaka stopped herself too late. "I am so sorry. I am so sorry—" she apologized.

Tehya laid a hand on her arm, "It is fine, Haaka. We know you were friends with Hakani. Please—you are welcome here."

Haaka just then realized who this was. *She is the one of whom Hakani was so jealous. This is the mate their Leader took after they thought she died. Oh, Hakani. She is so very nice—what were you thinking to hate her so?* And then it also hit Haaka that this was the female whom Akar'Tor had taken prisoner. *And here she is showing me such kindness, after being so terribly wronged by one raised among us.*

Oh'Dar changed the subject, "I had an idea for something new."

The females all turned in his direction. "We love your improvements, Oh'Dar. What is it now?" asked Tehya.

"I have been busy with it in my workshop," he said, "when I can get time alone in it, that is," he added, teasing the females who had taken it over. "I am surprised you have not seen it."

"We have not been there for a while, not since Arismae was born."

"After we finish eating, you must come and take a look. You too, Father. I could use some help moving it."

"What is it?!" Nimida exclaimed, patience not being one of her strong points.

"It is a present for Tehya—if she wants it. And then if you like it, we can also make one for you. Though I might need more supplies."

Haaka's eyes suddenly grew wide; she clutched Kalli close and pointed.

They all quickly turned to see what she was pointing at, then breathed a sigh of relief at recognizing Kweeuu, padding silently toward their table.

"That is Kweeuu, Haaka. He is like my offling." Then Oh'Dar remembered that Akar'Tor had asked when he saw Kweeuu if they were saving the wolf to "eat now or later?"

"We do not eat him, Haaka. That is very is important. He is my offling, and I love him. Do you understand?"

She looked at Oh'Dar as if he was mad but nodded slowly. The wolf looked like a pretty good food source to her, one it would be a shame to waste. He would feed an offling or two for a day or so. Though he presented no threat to her, the wolf could certainly hurt Kalli.

Oh'Dar shot his father a sideways glance. Acaraho nodded his head as if to say he would make sure no harm came to Kweeuu.

"Haaka," said Acaraho, "Oh'Dar is explaining that Kweeuu moves among us freely. He is important to us. He is a friend. He will not harm you or Kalli. You can ignore him, but if he bothers you, just tell him to go away."

"It listens to what you say?"

"Yes. Well, not always."

As if on cue, Kweeuu came to Oh'Dar's side. "Sit, Kweeuu," Oh'Dar said, and the giant grey wolf sat, panting and looking very much like he was smiling.

Having an audience, Oh'Dar put him through his paces. "Roll over. Spin. Play dead." Kweeuu did not disappoint Oh'Dar and was rewarded with a piece of raw meat.

So many wonders here, thought Haaka, though still cautious.

"So, you are not going to tell us what this surprise is?" Nimida asked Oh'Dar.

Nootau elbowed her and kidded, "You are always so impatient! He said we could see it after we eat."

Nimida pretended to sneer at Nootau, the brother she did not know she had. "Are we done eating yet? Can we go now?" she asked, and everyone laughed, including Tar, who was sitting next to her.

Finally, the meal was finished, and all except Haaka rose to follow Oh'Dar to his workshop.

"Are you not coming?" asked Oh'Dar, extending his hand to Haaka as he would as a courtesy to any female.

"You are including me?" she asked.

"Of course. If you want to, but if not, someone can take you and Kalli back to your quarters. But she seems content for now. Why not come along?"

Making sure that Kalli was still safely positioned, Haaka rose.

They all made their way down the long tunnel toward Oh'Dar's workshop. Haaka looked around her the whole way, noticing again how spacious the corridors and ceilings were. *Of course, this was originally the Mothocs' home; no wonder everything is so tall and wide.*

Acaraho moved aside for Oh'Dar to lead them in. Oh'Dar stepped in and then turned and pointed to his new creation. "There. What do you think?"

They filed in and stood looking at it. Adia looked at her mate. Nadiwani looked at Adia. Tehya looked at Khon'Tor.

"What is it?" asked Nimida.

At first, it almost looked like an animal; it was very long and quite bulky, made out of Bison hide. The stitching was done with thick hide of another type.

They all stood there, staring at it.

Oh'Dar went over and sat down on it.

"Ahhhhh," they exclaimed almost in unison and laughed.

"Oh. Let me try it," and Tehya removed Arismae from the sling and handed her to Adia. Then she hopped onto Oh'Dar's creation, sliding to the back as she had seen him do. She sat next to him and looked at the others. Her feet dangled, too high up to reach the floor.

"This is very comfortable. However did you think of it?" she asked Oh'Dar

"It seems like whenever I came to visit, you and Khon'Tor would be sitting on your sleeping mats propped up against the stone wall. I thought at one point that there had to be a more comfortable way. At first, I just made long stuffed pieces; they are over there," he explained, "but then I realized it all had to be fastened together to work. The Waschini have similar things; they call it furniture, though theirs is mostly hard and uncomfortable."

They turned to look at a row of long hide bolsters stacked against the wall, then back to Oh'Dar.

"It must have taken forever to make," said Adia.

"It has taken me quite a while. If I make another one, I will definitely ask for help."

"Is it heavy? It looks heavy," said Nadiwani.

"Yes! It is; that is why I needed my father here."

"Oh! I see now," laughed Acaraho. "I still remember hauling all these hides in to begin with, and now I get to haul *that thing* out of here?" he kidded.

"I think it is wonderful. Are you really giving it to me? To us?" Tehya asked.

"If you want it. If it is alright with Khon'Tor, of course."

Khon'Tor put on his sternest face, clasped his hands behind his back, and walked around it, looking it up and down from every direction. Everyone stopped and held their breath, not sure what was going on. Khon'Tor took his time, frowning the whole while. Tehya watched him, suddenly overcome again by how magnificent he was.

"Hmmph," he said and circled it another time.

For the first time in a very long while, Oh'Dar was worried. *Should I have asked him first? Oh no.*

"I think—" he said sternly, piercing Oh'Dar with his glare, "I think—it is a great idea, Oh'Dar," and he broke into a smile.

Everyone breathed an audible sigh of relief, and Tehya frowned at him from her position on the stuffed seat.

"Do not hurt yourself moving it, Acaraho," Khon'Tor kidded.

"Thanks. I will make sure not to," replied

Acaraho, knowing Khon'Tor realized very well that it would take both of them to move it.

Tehya smiled as she listened to the good-natured bantering being passed around the group.

"It is really big—are you sure it is going to fit?" asked Nimida.

"If any of you wants one, it would not have to be this big. I only made it this large because of Khon'-Tor's size."

"We will make room for it and then come get it in the morning if that is alright with you, Oh'Dar," said the Leader.

"But I do not want to get off," said Tehya, and they laughed again.

Haaka stood a little to the back of the others, taking it all in.

All of a sudden, Nimida looked around and asked, "Where is Tar?"

Tar had not followed the group. When they left down the corridor to the workshop, Tar slipped away to his quarters. *I appreciate being included, but I do not feel I belong with the group. They are the community Leaders, and I am not one of them.*

Back in her room, Haaka was lying on the sleeping mat, bouncing Kalli up and down and replaying the day's events. She thought about her arrival there and the warm greeting from the Healer and her Helper, Acaraho's generous provision of their temporary quarters, and the lighthearted exchange among the group at Oh'Dar's workshop. And Oh'Dar's creation. *I would never have thought of something like that. It does look comfortable. Being at Kthama is all so interesting, but overwhelming.* She had been glad to get back to her quarters.

Haaka suddenly wondered what Haan was doing. *Does he think of me? Even miss me, perhaps? I wonder if he will learn to care for me. It is too soon to expect him to be interested in mating. Hakani has not been gone very long. But then, Hakani said they only mated once. And it has been a very long time since Haan's first mate, Kesta, crossed over.*

Haan stood outside by the evening fire, warming his hands. The heat felt good on his sore palms. They had been busy clearing the area for their joining ritual. The time was drawing close.

"You seem less disturbed, Adik'Tar," said Artadel, Kayerm's Healer.

"I am. Knowing Kalli and Haaka are safe is a relief. And it spares any of our members having to look after them. We need all the numbers we can get. Have any more joined today?"

"No, but it is just as well. I do not know that I would trust anyone who wished to change sides at this point. It might well be with the intention of sabotage."

"So, the final count is forty?"

"Forty in all, counting Haaka," affirmed Artadel. Haan nodded and stirred the fire, realizing Kalli was not included in the count being so young and not being full Sassen.

Artadel looked up at the evening sky. "Not long now. We have only to set the stones."

They spent the rest of the evening in silence.

The next morning, Haan and his team traveled to the preparation spot and stopped abruptly. They stood in disbelief. The entire area had been destroyed.

Some of the smaller trees had been uprooted, the tops snapped off, and the trunks shoved top-down into the ground; others had been used as plows to tear up the groundwork. Giant stones that they were about to set in place had been split in two. Ruined.

"I know who did this. *Tarnor and his band*. They are trying to stop us from opening Kthama Minor. We can repair this in time, it looks worse than it is," said Haan, stepping carefully amid the deep ruts, toppled trees, and the boulders scattered around.

"We can repair the physical damage, but the energy we built up has been destroyed," said Artadel. He let out a huge sigh. "I will look for another area. Farther away, more secluded. Perhaps toward Kthama. It will take us longer to get there each time, but perhaps being closer to Kthama will turn out to be a benefit."

"This time, I will post sentries to make sure we are not followed." Haan hid his discouragement. *Perhaps this is part of the plan. Perhaps a delay is needed, and we do not yet know why.*

They returned to Kayerm to confront Tarnor and Dorn, the leaders of the resistance to the plan of opening Kthama Minor.

They found them outside, surveying wind damage to the roof of Kayerm's entrance.

"We found your handiwork," said Haan. "If you think that will stop us, it will not."

"I do not know what you are talking about," said Tarnor, raising his eyebrows.

"Do not play dumb. It is beneath even you, Tarnor," sneered Haan.

"Truly, *I do not know what you are talking about.* If you have an accusation, make it and stop wasting my time," spat Tarnor back at Haan.

"It is you who are wasting our time, with your *lies,*" and Haan shoved Tarnor backward with both his hands, almost causing the renegade to lose his balance.

Tarnor staggered, then turned around and picked

up a large, fallen tree limb. He came at Haan, swinging it with everything he had.

Haan ducked and felt a rustle in his hair as the huge branch swept past his head.

Tarnor regained his stance and swung at Haan again as Artadel stepped back from the fight. The Sassen code of honor did not allow two against one, and the two adversaries must be left to fight it out between themselves.

As the tree branch missed him again, Haan stepped forward, using the weight of the log's trajectory to push Tarnor to the ground. Haan leaped onto him, wrestling the branch out of his hand and tossing it away. Then the Leader straddled his opponent, his greater weight trapping Tarnor, and punched him in the face several times.

Tarnor raised his arms, instinctively defensive, but Haan wrapped his hands around Tarnor's throat and bore down with all his strength. Tarnor hammered his fists on Haan's forearms, trying to break his grasp, then he pulled his legs up and tried to push Haan off of him. When that did not work, he arched his back, trying to flip the Leader. It was all to no avail, Haan's superior weight and bulk had him pinned, and he was starting to lose consciousness.

Artadel stood by, realizing that if Haan did not stop, he would kill Tarnor. He weighed his options, uncertain if Haan meant to kill his adversary or not. There were only seconds to decide—would this be for the best, or would Haan later regret being the first to shed blood between the factions?

Artadel made his decision and roared out Haan's name. "Haan, stop. Enough. You have won. He is vanquished. Stop!" He stepped forward and grabbed one of Haan's arms, trying to loosen the grip.

Haan shrugged Artadel off, but it was enough to break him out of his blood lust. He released Tarnor's neck, panting with exertion and rage, and wiped his mouth.

As he climbed off Tarnor and stood shaking the dirt and leaves off himself, Haan shouted, "Next time, I will not spare you. Leave us alone. You can have Kayerm; there is no need for this. We can each move forward to the future of our own making."

Artadel stopped. "The future of your own making."

A chill seemed to pass through the Healer's very soul.

Tarnor dragged himself to his feet. "Whatever the krell happened to get you so upset, I wish I had done it. But I do not know what the *Rok* you are talking about."

"*Bacht*," spat Tarnor in Haans's direction. It was a terrible insult among the Sarnonn, and he stomped away only somewhat appeased.

Artadel turned to Haan. "What if he is telling the truth?"

"Who else would have done it, Artadel? Tarnor is lying; of course it was them." Haan started walking, ducking to avoid the branches that screened Kayerm's entrance.

Artadel was not going to contradict Haan in the state he was in, but it was clear that the Leader was not thinking clearly. *If he would stop and think about the size of the trees that were driven upside down into the ground—* "I will start looking immediately. Either way, we will not be ready by this full moon."

"It will be as it will be. But for now, I am going to Kthama, and you are coming with me."

Haan's sudden decision to go to Kthama had nothing to do with the destruction of their preparation site. He needed to talk to another Leader, someone on his level, and the only such ally he had was Khon'Tor.

Haan passed below the area where Akar'Tor had holed up with his prisoner, Tehya. He had no desire to go any nearer. He had tried to put Akar'Tor out of his mind. Having no idea of his adopted son's fate, he had surrendered him to the Great Spirit, whom Haan believed was the young male's only hope now for redemption—if Akar'Tor even still walked Etera.

This time it was First Guard Awan who came to tell Khon'Tor that he had a guest, finding him with Acaraho in the Great Chamber.

"The Sarnonn Leader is here," said Awan, "and another with him."

Khon'Tor was hopeful at hearing it was Haan, his first thought being that there might be some word of Akar'Tor. He and the High Protector followed Awan back to the Great Entrance.

Khon'Tor greeted the Sarnonn Leader and the Sarnonn standing next to him. "Come in. Do you wish to stay awhile?" He resisted the desire to ask him directly what the visit was about and did not take his eyes off the other male, waiting for an introduction.

"This is my Healer, Artadel," Haan finally volunteered. Can we go to one of your meeting rooms?"

Khon'Tor had become better at signing and speaking at the same time, and found this did help communication greatly—another of Oh'Dar's inspirations. "I would like Acaraho to join us. Whatever you are here to tell me, he should also know," and Khon'Tor signaled for Acaraho to walk with them.

Once they were all situated in the private room, Haan began to speak. "You know the area here at Kthama. I need a place for our people to prepare for the opening of Kthama Minor. The location we selected and had nearly ready was destroyed."

Both Acaraho and Khon'Tor had questions but sensed not to interrupt.

"It must be secluded, away from others, and with no chance of disruption. Perhaps it would be best if we are closer to Kthama; I should have thought of that to begin with. There is so much going on right now."

Since both Sarnonn were then silent, Acaraho spoke up, "How large an area, Haan, how many of you will there be?"

"There will be about forty of us. We will need a clear path to Kthama."

Both males sat thinking.

"The large meadow above Kthama, where the largest band of deer graze. It is sizeable and fairly close. There is a direct path up and down from there," said Acaraho to Khon'Tor.

"How long will you need to prepare it?" Khon'Tor asked Haan.

"If it is a meadow, then not much time. By the next full moon, we must be ready for the opening."

"Do you want us to post some of our guards to watch over it?"

"My people will do that. But your people will not see them. Do not worry."

"Nevertheless, we will tell everyone to stay away from that area. I hope you will someday explain how you do that, Haan, how they hide so perfectly. My people are well versed in hiding, yet your skills surpass ours by a great deal."

"Will you show me this place?"

"Would you like to see Kalli and Haaka before we do? I am sure Haaka would like to see you," said Acaraho.

"Yes. Then we must go and see the deer meadow." Haan turned to Artadel and told him to wait there.

When she heard the announcement stone clack

at the doorway, Haaka twirled around at the work-table where she, Adia, and Nadiwani had been sorting foodstuffs. Her eyes flew open as she saw Haan enter. "I did not expect to see you so soon. Is everything alright?"

"We need a new preparation place. Are you and Kalli doing well?"

"Yes, we are. Look at this Haan, it is a way of carrying Kalli easily, and she is very comfortable."

Haan inspected the sling that Haaka wore, turning her around to see the back.

"Hmmph," he said appreciatively.

Haaka tried to hand Kalli to him, but he put his hand up, "She is still too little. I might squash her."

"I understand how you feel, Haan. I am also afraid to hold my offspring. They look so fragile," agreed Khon'Tor.

Acaraho smiled inwardly, knowing Adia was seeded and that in time he would have one of his being sported about in such a wrap on Adia's hip.

Before they left, Haan put his arm around Haaka's shoulder and gave her an awkward hug.

Adia and Nadiwani stood in the background, both glad to see the interaction between the Sarnonn. They both sensed that Haaka had feelings for Haan, and from their viewpoint, it would be the perfect solution for the two to pair. Whether or not Haan returned her affections, though, was unclear—he was so occupied with other concerns it was hard to tell.

The four males left and made their way up to the meadow above. Haan surveyed the area, then closed his eyes for a moment. "This is perfect. And so much better than our first choice."

Artadel did the same and added, "The vortex is rich here."

"There is a small stream that runs through it, then, quite a way from here, it goes underground." Acaraho did not volunteer details that this was part of what fed the Gnoaii and the females' bathing area. He did add, "It is part of a water supply that we use inside."

"The Sassen will not foul the waters," said Haan, understanding that Acaraho was telling them not to use this particular water supply for bathing.

"I shall let my people know you will be here," said Khon'Tor. "This is an area the females sometimes use for offspring play, and the males use for games, but is not occupied much in the cooler weather. We leave it for the deer to graze."

"It has good energy; no wonder deer feel safe here." Haan was observing the herd scattered around, still sporting their darker winter coats. "The deer will adjust to our presence."

Soon, Haan and Artadel left, returning to Kayerm to assemble their followers.

Later that day, Khon'Tor called an assembly.

Once everyone was settled, he explained, "When the High Council was last here, I called you together and told you that the meeting was about the challenges facing us all and that in time I would explain more. As you are aware, we have made contact with the Sarnonn, a people we were not even sure still existed. Out of that contact have come some astounding discoveries about our past, one of which is the existence of a second cave system next to Kthama. This second system has been hidden from our knowledge for thousands of years. Now, because of the Sarnonn, we are about to discover its secrets, and hopefully, more information about both our past and theirs."

Khon'Tor waited while the murmuring wound down. "Over the next few weeks, preparation to open this second system, called Kthama Minor, will begin. As the time draws nearer, I will speak with you again. I believe this discovery will greatly assist us in furthering our understanding of our past, as well as helping us to make wise decisions moving forward into our collective futures. That is all. Thank you."

Khon'Tor was surprised that there were no questions, but the People had been through many bewildering challenges lately, and change came hard to the Akassa.

CHAPTER 3

Oh'Dar took out the gifts he had brought for Honovi, Ithua, and the others, looking them over and placing them in turn back in his saddlebag; he had steeled himself to return to the Brothers and face Acise.

His mother had asked if he wanted someone to go with him, but he needed to do this alone.

He changed into warmer wraps, hoisted the saddlebag over his shoulder, and went to get Storm.

The ride to the Brothers' village was brisk, and Oh'Dar lifted his face to the stinging cold. With the light covering of snow on the ground, he was careful not to let Storm run all out. Within a few months, Etera would wake, the snow would be gone, and spring would return.

He had not sent word ahead that he was coming, and the village was quiet for a change.

Isskel, one of the braves of Oh'Dar's age, was the first to see him approach and trotted over. He stopped and stood, appreciatively watching as Oh'Dar brought the stallion to a stand.

"Greetings, Isskel."

"Greetings, Oh'Dar. What a beautiful animal."

"Thank you. I am glad you reminded me, I need to tell the Chief that when the time is appropriate and if he would like, the Brothers may use him for stud." Oh'Dar looked at Isskel, wondering if he could be the brave whom Acise had chosen.

"Sounds like you are going to be here for a while, Oh'Dar. Your offer is a good deal for the Brothers. What do you want in return?"

Oh'Dar had forgotten that they did not like receiving anything for nothing. He tried to think of something not very valuable, but then realized that would be an insult. A stallion such as Storm was almost priceless. Then he remembered he had used one of the Bison hides for the chair he made for Tehya. Due to his large size, when Khon'Tor had the sickness, they had been brought back as coverings for him.

"A bison hide if anyone has one."

Isskel nodded, a big smile covering his face. "It is still a better deal for us; you need practice in negotiation!"

Grinning, Oh'Dar dismounted and removed his

saddlebag. The brave volunteered to take care of Storm and led the horse away.

Oh'Dar was almost afraid to look around, afraid to see *her*. His eye caught someone approaching, and he turned, relieved to see Ithua.

"What a nice surprise, Oh'Dar. Will you be staying?"

"For this visit, I only came to deliver some gifts. I brought presents for you and Honovi, Snana, and —Acise."

A pained expression crossed Ithua's face. "I would be glad to give it to her if you prefer not to see Acise."

Oh'Dar turned away for a moment, then without turning back to face Ithua, he asked, "Are they already bonded?"

"No. Not yet."

Oh'Dar felt a little better. *I do not know what difference it makes, though*, he thought.

"May I speak with you a moment, Ithua? I am not ready to face Acise yet."

"Of course. Come with me," she said.

Oh'Dar turned and followed the Medicine Woman into her shelter. He unpacked his bag and handed a beautiful woven pouch to her. She took it gingerly and looked back up at him.

"This is for you," he said.

Ithua carefully opened the pouch and pulled out a wooden comb, very much like the variegated one

Honovi had from the childhood she had spent among the Waschini.

"Oh, it is so beautiful," she exclaimed.

"Honovi already has a comb, so I brought her this," and he handed her another bundle, this one made of a soft velvety material. Ithua carefully unwrapped a looking glass, with a handle made of the same smooth wood as the comb. She startled when she held it up to herself. They had seen their reflections in ponds and puddles, but nothing as clear as this. She sat for a moment, transfixed. Her hand moved to her face as she watched herself touch her own cheek.

She lowered the mirror and said, "These are very generous, Oh'Dar."

He handed her three other wrapped bundles. "These are for the Chief and your brother. Careful, they are very sharp." She carefully unwrapped the knives Oh'Dar had chosen.

"There is also one for Noshoba when his father thinks he is old enough to have it," Oh'Dar added. He could almost read her mind—as beautiful as the gifts were, they were a sobering reminder at how more advanced the Waschini were in weapon-making.

Having accomplished what he meant to, Oh'Dar stood up.

"Please give the gifts to the others for me," he said.

"You have decided against seeing her?" asked Ithua.

"I struggle both ways. It is my fault I lost Acise." He paused. "It will only bother me more to know, but I have to ask anyway—who is it?"

"Pajackok," she replied.

Oh'Dar's heart sank. Pajackok was the only one regularly to best him at any sport. He was a fine man, very muscular, nearly as tall as Oh'Dar. Very handsome indeed. "He will be a great provider and protector. She will give him many healthy offspring," he said, repeating a common blessing of the Brothers.

"But he will never win her heart, Oh'Dar," Ithua said as he turned to leave, stopping him in his tracks.

"She does not love him?"

Ithua paused before continuing.

"She appreciates him. He is good to her. She sees his value as a partner. But from what I have seen, she does not love him, no."

"Why not?"

"Because her heart belongs to another," Ithua said softly.

For the first time, a glimmer of hope bloomed in Oh'Dar's heart. "But what of Honovi and Is'Taqa? Are they happy with the promise?"

"Pajackok is a fine brave. But he does not make their daughter's heart sing."

Unthinkingly, Oh'Dar ran his hand through the crown of his hair as he thought, an echo of Khon'-Tor's habit.

So, I have a chance, but I cannot give up. I must stand

by my choice. I could not wait to get here; this is home. I realize now that it is only guilt I feel about leaving my grandmother and Ben behind. This is where I belong. I could give Acise a good life, I know it.

"May I talk with Is'Taqa and Honovi? Alone?" he asked.

Ithua motioned for him to sit back down and left, returning after a while with Acise's parents.

"We did not know you were here, Oh'Dar. We are pleased to see you," said Honovi as they seated themselves.

"I brought you each gifts from the Waschini world. But that is not why I asked to see you. Forgive me for being blunt, but I understand Acise and Pajackok are not yet bonded."

Is'Taqa and Honovi looked at each other.

"That is true," said Is'Taqa.

"I love your daughter. I know I am late; I know it is my fault she chose another, but Ithua has given me hope that she might also care for me."

"So, you are remaining at Kthama?" asked Is'Taqa.

"Yes. No. Well, I have to go back to Shadow Ridge at some point. But this is my home. I know where I belong now, Is'Taqa. You have every right to doubt me, but I have made peace with myself and where I fit in, and who I am. I have accepted that I have a place, and I want to believe I have value to give to the People and the Brothers."

Honovi sighed. There was no doubt that Acise

was not over Oh'Dar and perhaps never would be. When Oh'Dar had stopped on his way through to Kthama, Honovi had watched her daughter come out of their dwelling, see him, and silently go back inside. Later, she could tell Acise had been crying, hard.

"There is no doubt her heart still belongs to you, Oh'Dar," Honovi finally admitted. "But you hurt her deeply when you rejected her," she added.

"We have watched you two since you became part of our family, Oh'Dar," said Is'Taqa. "The many seasons you spent with us learning our ways. There is a bond between you that I do not believe can be broken, and I am not sure she will truly be happy with anyone but you. But it is not as easy as simply taking back what you said when you left the last time."

"I know you only want what is best for her," said Oh'Dar. "I know I will never completely be one of you. I will never completely be one of the People. But I would do my best to care for her, provide for her, protect her, and make her happy."

"Ultimately, it is up to Acise," pointed out Is'Taqa. "It is she you must convince now, not us, Oh'Dar."

Oh'Dar was very happy to hear this; it seemed they approved of the match despite his complicated life.

"When are they to be bonded?" he asked.

"At the next full moon," said Honovi.

Oh'Dar's heart stopped. *I almost waited too long.*

"May I see her? And what of Pajackok?"

"Pajackok would be disappointed. But it is her choice. All the Brothers, like the People, honor the females' right to choose."

Honovi called out to Snana, whom she had heard eavesdropping outside the shelter. "Snana, go and fetch your sister. Do *not* tell her why and do not bring Pajackok if he is with her."

Oh'Dar's heart started pounding. He could not sit any longer and got up to stand near the entrance.

Within moments, Acise entered the shelter, pushed in by her younger sister. "Stop it," and Acise swatted back at Snana.

"Yes, Momma? Snana said you wanted to see me."

Is'Taqa indicated that Acise should look behind her, and she turned to find herself standing directly in front of Oh'Dar, looking up at those impossibly blue eyes.

"Oh," a sound escaped her lips, and her hand flew to her mouth. She turned back to her parents.

"What is he doing here? Momma, Papa, what is going on?" she was halfway between tears of anger and joy.

"I have come to declare my love for you, Acise," said Oh'Dar, placing his hand on her arm and gently turning her back to face him.

Acise frowned, and her eyes grew dark. "You left me. I did not know if you would ever return. You gave me no hope, Oh'Dar. I have moved on."

Oh'Dar could see she was angry and accepted that she had every right to be.

He took her hands in his and brought them up and pressed them to his cheek. "Forgive me, Acise. I should never have left you. I know I hurt you deeply, and I am so very sorry. I love you, and only you."

She snatched her hands away, and he clasped them again, this time gently kissing the tips of her fingers.

Still seated, her parents exchanged glances.

Once again, she pulled away. "Why should I forgive you? Just so that you can hurt me again?"

"Before I left, you told me you loved me. Surely your feelings have not changed so quickly? Please give me a chance to prove myself to you."

Acise threw back her arm to slap his face. He grabbed it mid-stroke and pulled her into him, bending her backward with a passionate kiss. She struggled, and he tightened his grip and kissed her harder.

He released her to let her catch her breath, and her dark eyes flashed at his. "Can you truly tell me that you no longer want to be with me?" he asked. When she did not answer, he kissed her again, and this time she did not struggle but relented and melted into him, returning his passion.

Snana looked overjoyed at the display.

Suddenly Acise pushed herself away from Oh'Dar, "No. No! You told me to move on, and I did. I am with Pajackok now. You cannot just ride in here and tell me you have changed your mind and that now you want me. You cannot treat me like this. *It is too late, Oh'Dar*. I will not let you hurt me again," and she stormed out of the shelter, her skirts whipping behind her.

Oh'Dar looked at Honovi and Is'Taqa, confused, "What just happened?"

"Give her a little while," counseled Honovi. "This is a shock for her. I know she loves you, but she is not over your leaving her. You cannot just expect an apology and a kiss to make her overlook how you treated her."

Oh'Dar plopped down next to Honovi. *I was sure she would forgive me. Now I do not know what to do. I cannot bear the idea of her with Pajackok.*

It was still early in the day, and Oh'Dar felt he had to do something. He finally rose. "I need to go back to Kthama. Would you ask Chief Ogima if he would be interested in using Storm for stud in the future when the mares come in season? I thought some different blood might be good."

"That is a thoughtful offer. Some new blood would no doubt be beneficial. Storm has traveled a long way; why not leave him here so Chief Ogima Adoeete can look at him. You can take Windrunner," said Is'Taqa.

"Windrunner? No, I cannot take the horse of the Second Chief," he exclaimed.

"Please do, he is getting out of shape, the ride to Kthama would do him good."

Oh'Dar relented because it would be rude to turn down the offer again. It was a huge sign of trust to let him take Is'Taqa's personal ride.

"Come, I will go with you to fetch him."

Is'Taqa and Oh'Dar walked over to where the horses and ponies were kept. Noshoba, Is'Taqa's son, was standing there talking to one of the braves and admiring Storm. As they approached, the brave turned to see who was coming.

Pajackok.

Pajackok looked about as happy to see Oh'Dar as Oh'Dar was to see him.

"Oh'Dar. We are admiring your stallion."

"I am leaving him here for a few days while I return to Kthama. He will not give you any trouble, though I do not suggest you try to ride him," cautioned Oh'Dar. "He is only accustomed to two riders."

"How long are you staying?" asked Pajackok, looking him up and down. Oh'Dar's hair had not yet grown much and was at an awkward length—not Waschini and not Brother.

"Congratulations on your upcoming bonding with Acise," he said, ignoring Pajackok's question, his voice lackluster.

Pajackok eyed the Waschini.

Is'Taqa separated Windrunner and led him away for Oh'Dar to mount. Pajackok and Noshoba exchanged looks. Is'Taqa never let anyone else ride Windrunner.

Oh'Dar mounted and turned the horse to say goodbye to the three standing there.

"I will be back in a few days," he said, and then urged Windrunner to head for Kthama.

Hidden in the bushes, Acise watched Oh'Dar ride off. She could not help but be impressed at how he handled Windrunner. She also was surprised that her father had let him ride the stallion. It was unheard of. For some reason, it bothered her that her father had done Oh'Dar such an honor.

Good, he is gone. Now I can get back to my life. I need to keep moving forward. Soon Pajackok and I will be bonded, and I will forget all about the Waschini with the blue eyes. Oh'Dar had long disappeared before Acise finally left her hiding place.

Oh'Dar returned to Kthama and looked for his father. He needed to talk to someone about what had happened. He found Acaraho outside with a few of his workers, pointing up at some rubble that had started to give way over Kthama's entrance.

Acaraho turned as he heard the hoofbeats approach, surprised to see Oh'Dar on what looked like Is'Taqa's stallion.

He waited for his son to dismount before asking, "Is that not Windrunner?"

"Yes. Is'Taqa loaned him to me; I am leaving Storm there with them for a few days."

"I see. Did you accomplish what you went there to do?" Acaraho asked.

"Well, I need to talk to you, Father."

Acaraho excused himself, brows raised.

"I talked to Is'Taqa and Honovi about Acise. They said she still loves me. Then I talked to her. I told her that I should never have left without telling her that I loved her."

"And then what happened?"

"I kissed her. And then she became angry and told me it was too late, she was promised to Pajackok—and stormed off."

Acaraho thought a moment, trying to place Pajackok. "I have heard Is'Taqa speak of him. Pajackok is a good choice. He will be a good provider."

"Whose side are you on?" exclaimed Oh'Dar, screwing up his face.

"Come—sit down. What did you expect, Oh'Dar? You have acted erratically with her. From everything I know, she has little reason to trust you."

"Well, no. I guess not. I have been inconsistent."

"Females need security, Oh'Dar. They have to know that our love for them is not just a *passing fancy* —is that what you called it? They give us their hearts, attention, love, offspring. And over all the years of doing this, they also give us their youth. They need to know we want to be with them because of who they are, not just because they are young and pretty, and for a season in their lives draw all the males' eyes."

"Is that what she thinks? That this is just an infatuation? Something I will get over?"

"You did leave her. Males do not usually leave females they cannot live without. From her point of view, she has reason to doubt you," Acaraho said as kindly as possible. "And I also remember that she was the one pursuing you, and not the other way around. You said that you told her to move on, that you did not know where you belonged. You cannot blame her for believing you. Your leaving just confirmed for her that you cannot be counted on to stay in her life."

Acaraho paused a moment, seeing Oh'Dar was struggling.

"Son, when you left, you let her think you were over her—that you could forget her, and she should forget you."

"Are you saying I have to prove myself to her?" Oh'Dar thought for a moment. "How am I going to do that? I am not around enough. And they are to be bonded soon."

"As long as you are out of sight, she can tell herself she is over you. And maybe she is—but if that is true, you need to find out for sure. And you cannot do that from here."

"But they are to be bonded soon," he said. "At the next full moon."

"Well, then I would not waste any more time here," Acaraho smiled.

Oh'Dar remembered how Jenkins had told him to give Miss Blain something to remember him by. *What I gave Acise to remember me was a broken heart. And by leaving, I opened the door for someone else to step in, to step in and be everything I have not been—dependable, reliable, a part of her life day after day—everything Father just told me females need. What have I been by comparison? Someone who drops in and out of her life without warning.*

"Thank you, Father. I think I know what I have to do. I am going to pack some things and go back to the Brothers' village. Please tell Mother I may be gone for a while."

Acaraho nodded and patted Oh'Dar on the shoulder.

Oh'Dar hurried into Kthama to gather what he needed, "It will only take me a few moments."

True to his word, Oh'Dar did return quickly. Acaraho watched his son mount Windrunner.

"If you really love her and she is the one for you, do not come back without winning her heart, son," and Acaraho watched Oh'Dar ride away toward the female he loved. Once he was out of sight, Acaraho went to find Adia to tell her what had happened.

Oh'Dar pulled into the Brothers' village just as Honovi and Acise were preparing the evening meal.

Acise looked up in horror. "What is he doing back?"

Honovi smiled to herself. *Good move, Oh'Dar.*

"What are you doing here?" demanded Acise as he rode toward them. Water could have been turned to ice by the tone in her voice.

"I brought some things I will need. I am staying for a few weeks, and then later, I hope I will be back to stay through the summer. I am sure your father has a lot of work I could help with, and I have projects of my own to complete," he said. "But I know where I belong now, Acise, and if I can give you reason to forgive me, it is here with you, the Brothers, and the People." And he continued by on Windrunner.

"*Momma!*" said Acise.

"I am sorry, Acise. But Oh'Dar has always been like a part of our family," she answered. "I do not see how we can reject him now."

"Where will he be staying? Certainly not with us," she exclaimed.

"He always stays with us, Acise. But do you want me to make other arrangements for him to stay with another family?"

Acise looked at her mother and stomped away without answering, not sure where to go, but knowing she did not want to be there any longer.

Before she knew where she was headed, she

found herself standing next to Windrunner with her father, her brother Noshoba, and Oh'Dar.

"You cannot be serious," she said, facing Oh'Dar, hands on her hips

"Acise, what is wrong?" her father asked.

"Oh'Dar said that he is staying through the whole summer. That he wants to help you with your work, and he has work here that he needs to do for himself. And Momma says he is staying with us in our shelter."

"I am not sure what is going on, but I am not getting in the middle of it. Oh'Dar has always been welcome here, and he always will be," Is'taqa said, trying to be as noncommittal until he could talk to Honovi.

"Do you not need to get back to Shadow Land, or whatever that place is?" Acise glared at Oh'Dar.

"Shadow Ridge."

"Shadow World," she said, to irritate him.

"Shadow *Ridge*. It is called Shadow *Ridge*. Yes, someday. But Kthama is my home, and I have some projects I need to complete to help my people," Oh'Dar said. "And maybe I can convince you to forgive me for being a fool earlier and turning you away."

Acise glared at him.

Realizing that he would get no reply, Oh'Dar turned to Is'Taqa.

"Thank you for letting me use Windrunner. He did well. I do see what you are saying; he has put on some weight since I was here last. I think the trip to Kthama and back did him good. Perhaps tomorrow we can talk about how I can help you this summer."

Acise stood there, hands still on her hips, watching her father and Oh'Dar talking. Noshoba walked over to join his sister. "Oh'Dar is staying a while?"

"It appears so."

Noshoba's face brightened. "Then, he will be here for your bonding ceremony with Pajackok."

The color drained from Acise's face.

That evening, Oh'Dar sat around the family fire with Is'Taqa, Honovi, Snana, and Noshoba as he had so often over the years. Acise, however, had not joined them.

"Where is Acise?" asked Snana, always ready to tease her sister.

"I think she is in the shelter. Noshoba, go and bring your sister here," said Honovi.

A little while later, Noshoba returned without Acise. "She said she is not feeling well; she has already turned in."

"So—what are we working on this summer, Oh'Dar?" asked Is'Taqa.

"Khon'Tor's mate, Tehya, has sparked an interest among the females of wearing different wrap designs. They have taken over my workshop," he laughed. "I want to replenish the materials they have used up. Honovi, if you do not mind, I need your help in making that lightweight, gauzy material you weave. I know that in the warmer months, they will enjoy working with it. And also whatever hides I can manage to prepare."

"That sounds good. I always enjoy your company," said Is'Taqa.

"Oh, and Khon'Tor has not asked, but I would like to gather some more stones for another neck string for Tehya. Maybe you could help me with that, Snana, Noshoba?" asked Oh'Dar as he wrapped his arm around the young boy and smiled at Snana.

After Noshoba had been sent to bed, they sat at the fire a while longer, passing the time until it was late enough to turn in. Is'Taqa stayed to put out the fire while the others filed into the shelter.

It was roomy enough for all of them. Is'Taqa had built it in expectation of an extended family with lots of grandchildren.

Honovi had rolled out a blanket for Oh'Dar in his usual place, and once he had settled in, he looked around to see Acise on the far side of the shelter—nowhere near her customary place closer to him.

Acise lay still as a rock, feigning sleep.

Morning found her still awake. As she saw her mother rise and step outside, Acise rose quietly to join her.

"Momma, Oh'Dar cannot stay here," she said, trotting to catch up.

"I understand. I will ask your father to find another family for him to stay with. But you must make peace with his being in our village, Acise, and if you are sure you do not want to be with him, put him out of your mind. Pajackok is a fine choice; he is one of our most highly-skilled braves. You will be bonded before long, and I am sure he will give you many fine offspring. In fact, we need to get to work on your ceremonial dress."

Acise stood staring at her mother, lost in thought.

Oh'Dar woke up and stretched. Noshoba and Snana were still sleeping, but he could see that Honovi, Acise, and Is'Taqa must already have woken. He straightened out his sleeping blanket, put on his heavier outer wraps, and stepped outside.

Seeing Hononvi and Acise talking by the fire pit, he went to find Is'Taqa. Acise noticed Oh'Dar leave the shelter and stared after him as he walked away.

Honovi watched as her daughter's eyes followed Oh'Dar. *It is obvious she still loves him; otherwise, she would not be upset at his being around. She will be miserable if she goes through with Pajackok. It does not matter that Pajackok would be a fine provider. It does not matter that he is the most skilled brave in the village. He will never have her heart. We must help her get over her pride before she makes a mistake she will regret the rest of her life.*

CHAPTER 4

Haan's team had completed the limited physical preparation needed for the meadow above. Herds of deer watched from a safe distance within the tree line, waiting to reclaim the rich resource.

A ring of giant rocks had been moved and set in place, twelve in all—though more than twelve Sarnonn would be participating in the ritual. The ground within the circle had been pounded flat under the many feet of Haan's people as they made their preparations. Part dance, part meditative movement, they had begun building the energy in the meadow—regaining the progress that had dissipated in the destruction of the first site. As they moved in pattern, circles of giant bodies intertwining in a complex ritual, they once again chanted words that been unspoken for generations. Sacred words, forbidden words, words that created vibrations designed to awaken the dormant forces harnessed by the Mothoc more than an age ago.

The sealed entrance to Kthama Minor had stood undisturbed for generations, its secrets safe, waiting until it would be forced to give up its mysteries. Inside something was waiting—waiting to be awakened from a long slumber.

Deep inside the corridors of Kthama, Adia and Urilla Wuti felt a shift. A feeling of discomfort overcame them both, one they did not recognize, had never experienced before.

"What is that?" asked Adia.

"I do not know. But something tells me this is just the beginning of it. And only the very tip of it as well."

"I do not like it. It makes me nervous—a little overwhelmed, anxious. I am not sure how to describe it. As if something is trying to get inside—"

"—or out."

"Yes—but inside or outside of what? If I did not know better, I would think it was inside myself, but that cannot be," said Adia.

"Let us practice strengthening our perimeters," suggested Urilla Wuti.

So they took their places on their respective mats and began the exercises designed to help them block outside energies. Though, outside and inside seemed to be meaningless terms in the realms within which they were working. These were realms where there was no inside or out, no here, or there. Everything existed at a level where there was only the One. They were working to create separation where separation was impossible. The harder Adia tried to understand it, the more success slipped past her reach. This was not the realm of understanding—the Great Spirit's aspect of Reason. It was not the realm of love or emotion—the Great Heart. Here they were working in the realm of the Great Spirit known as the Great Will, and it was work that required the soul's intention.

Lifrin had passed onto them an understanding of the One-Who-Is-Three, which had opened their minds to the work they had to do to survive the opening of Kthama Minor. Beyond the completion of that event, these practices would strengthen all their Healer abilities, and if they survived, would propel them both to further their skills more than could otherwise have been achieved in their lifetimes.

Adia brought her intention into focus. She visualized it as a thin edge surrounding her and everything that mattered to her. Then she focused it tighter, harder, finer. Once it was the thinnest boundary possible—a hair's breadth, perhaps—the goal was to expand it while never losing its fine, concentrated quality. The trick was enlarging it without allowing the strength and edge of her intention to become diluted or dissipated as she expanded it. Everything she had experienced told her that as something was stretched or enlarged, it was also weakened. Her mind had to let go of this understanding so that her intention could succeed. Where her mind and her intention conflicted, she had to set aside her natural understanding of how things worked.

This is the struggle of all our souls' journeys, she thought. *Bringing into harmony the three aspects of the Great Spirit—the mind, the emotions, the will. Where there is conflict between our reason or understanding, our feelings, and our intentions, we are out of balance within ourselves. Peace, connection, and effectiveness are thwarted. The Great Spirit imbued us with each of its own attributes. What it achieves without effort, that being its very nature, we struggle to do within ourselves for our entire lives.*

My father told me I needed to achieve balance. That my Great Heart could not always lead, that I needed to develop my reasoning so it could work together with my feelings to provide balance and perspective. No, is that right? Maybe it is not quite. It is not about developing my understanding—because it is not my understanding. I must learn to listen to the voice of understanding from the Great Spirit. Yet how can I do that when my heart is drowning out everything else?

Feeling Adia's intention stream dissipate, Urilla Wuti broke her concentration and said, "What are you doing, Adia?"

"I am sorry. I was thinking," Adia apologized.

Urilla Wuti sighed. "Are you ready to try again?"

"Yes. But it is so hard. And I am afraid we are running out of time."

"Set aside the voice of your feelings. Set aside the

voice of your need to understand. This is the work of our will, our intention. Like any other skill Adia, we simply need to practice. When your stream dissipated, I felt it. Somehow, we are joined together in this, and it will take both of us to succeed. I now understand Lifrin, and why I am here with you at Kthama."

Adia repositioned herself so that nothing physical was disturbing her. She engaged her intention, closed her eyes, and began again.

Her inner eye could see the boundary she was creating. She could see it honed into a fine, sharp-edged field of incredible focus and power. She pictured expanding it, but again, as it expanded, it diluted. *No. That is an illusion, a lie. Change is an aspect of time —there is no change in the realm of what already is.* She switched perspective. Instead of willing it to expand, she simply accepted that it was larger. There was no process of expansion; in that second, there was only a thicker boundary—still focused, powerful, imbued with vibrational power.

Urilla Wuti let out an involuntary gasp and opened her eyes to look at Adia. "What did you do differently just now?"

Adia came out of her state to answer the other Healer. "I was trying to move toward it, trying to create a stronger boundary. When I stopped striving to create it through a process of change and just willed it, I succeeded. Learning about this is fascinating, but it would be more enjoyable if we had more time." *And if I were not worried about being seeded.*

"Nadiwani does not seem to be able to do any of this, Urilla Wuti," she added as she thought through her list of concerns.

"No, but remember she does not have as high a seventh sense. So perhaps that is its own protection."

"I think I am done for this morning; some of my earlier unease is gone. How about you?" asked Adia.

"Yes, I do not feel it as strongly, either. I take it as proof that what we are doing is working. I am retiring to my quarters, where I will practice a bit more."

Acaraho passed As Urilla Wuti left. "Is my mate in there?" he asked.

"She is resting because we just completed a session. But I am sure she would want to see you, Commander."

Acaraho thanked Urilla Wuti and entered quietly in case Adia was asleep. She looked up as he came in and smiled.

"Join me?" she suggested, patting a place beside her on the mat.

Acaraho sat down next to her. "Oh'Dar went to deliver the gifts he brought from the Waschini world, and to face Acise."

"How did it go?"

"From what he described, he made his intentions clear. But, it seems Acise is not ready to believe him yet. He hurt her before, and she still has doubts about the permanence of his interest in her. She is still promised to Pajackok, so he has returned to the village to stay for a while."

"Your suggestion?"

"Yes. I think Acise is justified in how she feels. If Oh'Dar wants to win her, he has to prove himself, and he cannot do it from Kthama."

Adia sat quietly. "The Brothers have different expectations about mating. I know they allow experimentation among their young adults. I hope that Acise and Pajackok have not yet physically joined," she mused.

"If they have, I hope she would tell him. I believe that for Oh'Dar, that would be hard, though. It is one area where our cultures are very different," said Acaraho.

"I hope he returns before Haan and his followers open Kthama Minor. I do not know what aftermath to expect," worried Adia.

"Did something happen?"

She sighed. "Yes, something happened. Both Urilla Wuti and I felt a shift this morning. It was not pleasant, but we worked to strengthen our boundaries, and that helped."

Acaraho frowned. "I know you said leaving the area would not help, but I am worried, Adia."

"I understand, Saraste'. But I believe in provision,

and we were benefited greatly by the knowledge Lifrin shared—which originally came from Oh'Dar's joke, remember? About going back in time to talk to her?"

"Oh'Dar has had a great effect on this community. Not just the innovations, but his help with the sickness, and just recently his saving Tehya—and her offspring when she stopped breathing after she was born."

Adia thought back to Khon'Tor's wrath over her bringing a Waschini offspring into Kthama and his prediction that Oh'Dar would bring only problems to the People. *"The presence of the offspring creates a danger to all the People. He is an encumbrance. He is weak and frail. He will never be able to function as a contributing member of our community. He will never be allowed to leave; he will spend the rest of his life here. What will become of him when he reaches pairing age? When he is filled with a male's natural desires? None of the females will have him. He is pitiful. And repulsive. He will never be a provider or a protector. He will live and die alone—separated from his kind—that is the life to which you have sentenced him, Adia. That is the life you have condemned him to—"*

"Yes, not the future that Khon'Tor predicted for him," she whispered. "How is Khon'Tor doing, Acaraho? After what happened with Tehya and Akar'Tor—"

"He is distracted. Deep in thought, I can tell. On top of Tehya's kidnapping and the opening of

Kthama Minor, Akar'Tor still has not been found—"

"I am worried about Khon'Tor; we came close to losing him forever. I think it is time I talked to him again. And to Tehya. I will go and find them after I have rested."

When Khon'Tor came in, Tehya lay stretched out on the overstuffed hide seating that Oh'Dar had made. Acaraho and Khon'Tor had wrangled it into their quarters after making the space, and it quickly became one of the favorite features of their living area. Tehya had named it the *softsit*.

She sat up as Khon'Tor approached, making room for him to be seated. He took her into his arms and held her.

"You have been so busy lately, and I have missed you so much. Oh, Khon'Tor, please never leave me." She buried her face and her fingers in his chest hair.

"I will never leave you, Tehya."

"*But you almost did*. You almost killed yourself. What would I have done without you? What kind of life would that have left me—yearning and grieving for you the rest of my life? Raising our daughter alone, her never knowing her amazing father."

"You would have found another, Tehya. You are too beautiful and sweet to be alone," he whispered, anger stirring at the thought of it.

"You still do not understand. There will never be —*can never be* another. There is no one like you. I would have spent the rest of my life alone and heart-broken. Your *solution* to saving me would have destroyed me. Why can I not make you understand what you mean to me, what our life together means to me? The fact that you think I would ever be with another tells me you do *not* understand the depth and breadth of my love for you."

He pulled her in close and held her. *I need to tell her about my past. Until she knows, I will always fear losing her.*

"Tehya, I have done some terrible things. I have done things no one had a right to. If you knew, it would change how you feel about me—and so I must tell you because you still have time to find happiness with someone worthy of you."

"Please stop saying this. I do not care what you have done. There is nothing you can tell me that will change how I feel about you. *Nothing.*"

"You say that because you do not know. Once I tell you about my past, then if you still feel the same, I will believe you," said the Leader.

"Then tell me, Khon'Tor, so we can get past this."

When she used his name instead of her usual playful Adoeete, he knew she was serious.

"Not now. Not at this moment. But soon, I prom-ise," he said. *Why am I putting it off? Because I am certain that I will lose her. And I want a few more days of happiness with her—to remember. What will I do after Tehya is gone? She will take Arismae and go back to Far High Hills, taking with her my heart and everything that matters to me. All that I cherished before—power, position, control—none of it matters. And everything I did not value before but do now will be taken from me as the price for learning too late that it is what truly matters.*

Their privacy was interrupted by someone at their door. Without entering, the guard called into the room that the Healer was there to see Khon'Tor.

"Please tell her I will locate her later. It is not a good time," Khon'Tor answered.

"Yes, Adik'Tar," the guard said.

Outside the door, Adia's concern rose. She could feel sadness, fear, anxiety, remorse, regret—a broad swathe of negative energy radiated from the room. *They need help. They both need help to get through this. What terrible timing, with everything else going on—if only they had found Akar's body, that would go a long way to resolving at least part of this.* She turned away, saying a prayer to the Great Mother for inspiration.

As she walked back down the corridor, Adia realized that she was still affected by the emotions that had emanated from Khon'Tor's quarters. *I am so much more sensitive now. I thought the exercises were supposed to help with that.* She stopped for a moment and tried strengthening her boundaries, which did help dissipate the distress she was receiving from both Khon'Tor and Tehya.

Acise and Pajackok were another day closer to being paired.

"May I join you?" A voice broke the evening silence.

Oh'Dar looked up to see his rival towering over those who were seated around the evening fire.

"Of course," answered Honovi, moving over to make room between herself and Snana.

"Where is Acise? Is she not joining you this evening?" Pajackok asked as he lowered himself to sit.

"She has taken to staying in the shelter during the evenings."

Pajackok looked across at Oh'Dar, suspecting his presence was the reason. The firelight accentuated Oh'Dar's differences from the Brothers—differences that only seemed to make him mysterious. "How long are you staying, Oh'Dar?" he asked.

"I will be here for a couple of weeks; then I will return home for a while. But I plan on spending most of the summer here. I have a lot of work to do, and I want to help Is'Taqa and Honovi if I can."

"You do not need to trouble yourself with that; I will be glad to help them. I will be part of the Second Chief's family soon."

Is'Taqa and Honovi exchanged fleeting glances. Tension was building.

"May I go and see Acise?" asked Pajackok.

"Of course," said Is'Taqa, looking over at Oh'Dar as he did. The briefest frown crossed Oh'Dar's face as he watched Pajackok head for the family shelter.

After a while, Oh'Dar stood up.

"I would not do that, son," warned Is'Taqa.

Oh'Dar tossed down the stick he had been poking the fire with and kicked at some stones, then turned back to face them. A terrible image crossed his mind—of Acise and Pajackok alone together in the shelter.

"Honovi. Have they—?"

"No, Acise would have told me if they had. This, I know."

"*What are they doing in there?*"

"They are just talking. Sit back down. Try to think of something else," advised Is'Taqa.

Acise was lying on her blanket, facing the outer wall, affording herself a small amount of privacy for her thoughts. She did not hear Pajackok enter and only noticed when someone sat down next to her, placing a hand on her hip.

She startled, quickly turning over.

"What are you doing here?" she asked, now realizing she had been avoiding him since Oh'Dar arrived.

"I have not seen you for a while, Acise. Are you alright?" asked Pajackok.

"Yes. Why would I not be?" she said.

"I have not seen you since Oh'Dar returned."

"I have been busy; that is all."

"We will be bonded soon. I thought perhaps we might—there is no real reason to wait," said Pajackok, running his hand over the curve of her hip and down the outside of her thigh.

"It is not that long, Pajackok. We have come this far; we can last a while longer."

Pajackok withdrew his hand and abruptly turned his back to her.

"I do not know what you see in him. He is a good archer, and he can ride with the best. But he is not one of us, even when the summer sun darkens his skin, and he never will be. He never stays put. You and I have known each other all our lives, Acise; I can be a good provider for you. I know I can make you happy."

"Who are you talking about?" she sat up to face him.

"Do not play games. Time is running out. I know you have feelings for Oh'Dar. When you were little, they were just a child's infatuation. But now that you are a woman, I know it has grown into more than that."

"I am not playing a game. We are to be paired in a

few weeks. Let it go," said Acise, and she lay back down and rolled away from him.

Pajackok jumped up and stormed out of the shelter, making a beeline back to the firepit.

"Why did you come back here, Oh'Dar?" he shouted, arms out wide.

Oh'Dar was on his feet in seconds.

"What is the problem, Pajackok? I told you why I came back here."

"You came back here for her—admit it!" he stepped forward and shoved Oh'Dar in the chest.

Is'Taqa stood up, not to interfere, but prepared to make sure things did not get out of hand.

"Alright, I do not deny it," shrugged Oh'Dar. "But what business is that of yours?"

"What business is it of *mine*? You know we are to be bonded."

"You are not bonded yet, Pajackok."

"Leave, or I will make you leave!" Pajackok stepped forward and shoved Oh'Dar once more.

"Do not do that again, Pajackok. My patience only goes so far."

"Or what? Will you fight me? I will be glad to fight you, Oh'Dar. The first to draw blood wins—the loser leaves here and never returns."

Is'Taqa stepped between the two young bucks.

"No one is fighting anyone, and no one is leaving. Pajackok, you are not thinking clearly. What if you lost? Are you prepared to leave your father and mother? Your family? Never to see them again?"

"I do not intend to lose," and Pajackok glared at Oh'Dar, fists clenched.

Oh'Dar ripped both his heavy tunic and under-cover off over his head, and slammed them into the dirt to the side, revealing a rippling physique. "*Neither do I,*" he threatened, leaning forward, tensing his muscles.

A shadow of hesitation crossed Pajackok's face as he looked his opponent up and down.

Hearing raised voices, Acise came out of the shelter. She could see Pajackok and Oh'Dar facing off, lit by the fire's glow. "*Stop it! Stop it!*" she shouted as she scurried over to them, putting her arms out as if to separate them. "Pajackok, what are you doing?" she yelled.

"Getting rid of this interloper," he snarled in Oh'Dar's direction, never taking his eyes off of him.

"Oh'Dar is not an interloper."

"He does not belong here. The sooner he leaves, the better. "

Acise's eyes flashed. "What am I? Some bone two wolves are fighting over? If I remember correctly, the female chooses who she wants to be bonded with."

Pajackok turned to frown at her. "You have already chosen. What do you care if Oh'Dar stays or leaves?"

"It is not that simple, Pajackok,"

Pajackok turned on Oh'Dar. "This is all your fault." He lunged at the Waschini, knocking both of them to the ground. Before anyone could interfere, the two were rolling around in the dirt. Feet and hands became a blur as the two men struggled. Without a shirt, Oh'Dar had the advantage as there was less for Pajackok to grab hold of other than his legging wraps. Oh'Dar had the height advantage and used it to try to flip Pajackok onto his back. Somewhere in the background, a woman's voice registered, screaming for them to stop, just before they were both doused with ice-cold water.

"What the—" the freezing water immediately broke up the fight. The two young men sprang apart, each on his feet in seconds as water dripped off their soaked forms.

They looked over to see Honovi holding an oversized water basket, now empty.

"Now you two will stop it immediately. Pajackok, go home. Oh'Dar, calm down or go back to Kthama. No one is fighting anyone. Acise is right—it is her choice to make. And until she does, the promise between her and Pajackok is null."

She turned to her daughter.

"You need to make up your mind. Get over your pride; this is the rest of your life. Search your heart and decide—perhaps the choice is not which of these men you want to live with, but rather, which of them can you not live without?"

Pajackok scowled, still furious. Oh'Dar, feeling the same, never took his eyes off of the brave.

"Go, now," said Is'Taqa. "You too," he said to

Acise. "You can stay with Ithua tonight. It will give you some time to think."

Acise watched Pajackok stomp off, then glanced at Oh'Dar before she left. She tried to block out how handsome he was, standing there dripping in the firelight, the shadows emphasizing everything about him that made him so mesmerizing. *What is it about him? Is it just his physical attractiveness? I cannot build a lifetime on that. Momma is right; this is a huge decision—perhaps the biggest one I will ever make. Pajackok is a better fit, but can I get the Waschini out of my heart? I am angry with him for leaving me, but pairing with Pajackok to punish Oh'Dar would have disastrous consequences for all of us. And it would be childish.*

"Alright, Momma. I will gladly stay with Ithua tonight. I will be back in the morning," she said and walked away, lost in thought.

Ithua had been watching from across the village. Nearly every other family had turned in, so she had a clear view of her brother's family fire. Ithua did not need to overhear what was being said to understand what was going on. She was glad to see her niece headed her way.

She came out and wrapped a warm woven shawl around Acise, inviting her into her space. "Sit down, child. Rest."

"Did you see what happened?"

"Yes. I am glad you are here. You need to let everything settle a while before you figure out what you want."

"Momma said I need to figure out not which one I want to live with, but which one I cannot live without."

"Your mother is wise. Regret is a hard master. You can only choose one man, Acise. You must decide between them, and when you do, no doubt you will lose the other from your life forever," she said. "Once your choice is made, your journey cannot easily be turned."

Acise looked at her, horrified. "I had not considered that, do you mean both Pajackok and Oh'Dar could leave?"

"Well, it is possible, though it is doubtful. Both have ties here, family ties. No. I mean that whoever you choose, the other will move on. Whichever man you do not choose will realize he has lost the battle forever and will make a life for himself, either alone or with another woman."

Ithua could see that Acise had not thought past the moment to the consequences of her choice. "In your imagination, when you picture the one you did not choose walking away, you picture him as stopping and turning to look back at you because you are still in his heart. That is a normal daydream. But instead, once you have chosen, you must visualize that the other will no longer stop and look back. You must envision that he will accept another woman's hand and continue with her as his life-walker. But lie down now. You are not to be bonded with Pajackok for a few weeks. There is time to figure this out.

"No, Momma vacated the promise. There is no date now for our bonding."

Ithua searched Acise's face, looking for relief—or sadness. In the darkness, she could not tell.

Honovi is even smarter than I realized, she thought to herself. Ithua had never taken a partner, and her thoughts returned to a time long ago, when she had been faced with a similar choice. Only hers was not between two men, but whether to bond or not, and in the end, she had chosen not to bond. But the brave she loved and had turned away was never far from her thoughts. She was grateful for the dark, which hid the tears tracing a path down her cheeks.

Ithua rolled out a sleeping blanket for Acise. "Here, lie down now," she repeated and covered Acise with another blanket.

In the dark, she could hear Acise's stifled sobs.

Back at the fire, no one was speaking. Eventually, Honovi shooed Snana into the shelter and carried a sleeping Noshoba in after her. Oh'Dar, now dried off by the flames, helped Is'Taqa extinguish the evening fire.

"I am sorry, Is'Taqa. My being here is a bad idea."

"I would not say that, Oh'Dar. As I said, both her mother and I know that Acise has feelings for you, and has for a long time. We both hope your staying here will help her decide once and for all. We have watched you struggle with where you belong. Honovi has had her own struggles, being half Waschini. There is no way to avoid tension between you and Pajackok."

"Yes, but I did not expect it to escalate like this."

"No one has been harmed, and I plan to keep it that way," said Is'Taqa. "It had to come to a head. And now that it has, she needs time to make a decision—one she can live with. I just hope she chooses as wisely as her mother did."

It took Oh'Dar a moment to get the joke, and then he laughed out loud. "It is not fair of me to ask, but who do you hope she chooses, Is'Taqa?" Oh'Dar asked.

"I hope she chooses whichever of you makes her heart sing. The one whose face she searches for above all others. The one who makes her blood race when she thinks of him, whom she would be proudest to stand next to. The man she can look up to for counsel, support, kindness. He whom she would choose to be father to her offspring. That is the one whom I hope she chooses."

"A fair and wise answer. I would have to say, that is the man I also hope she chooses. She deserves to be happy. If I am not the one who can give her that, then I hope she chooses another. I would hate to rob her of all the joy that being bonded to the right one can bring."

Is'Taqa looked at the tall Waschini. *I just hope she is wise enough to know which one of you that is*, he thought to himself, *because to me the choice is very clear.*

The next morning, Oh'Dar and Is'Taqa went about their plans. Now that the bonding was off indefinitely, Oh'Dar could have made a trip back to Kthama. But he was not going to. He needed to see this through, and he knew that leaving was the wrong thing to do. Besides, his father had told him not to come back without winning her, and Oh'Dar took that as a large vote of confidence that he was the one she belonged with—at least in his father's mind.

Oh'Dar and Noshoba moved the brushes over Storm and Windrunner, though neither horse needed grooming. But it was calming and enjoyable work and increased the bond between horse and rider.

"Do you think I could ever ride Storm?"

"I do not know, Noshoba. He only accepts two people so far. But there is a good chance you could ride his colt or filly someday when you are older."

"I hope she picks you, Oh'Dar," Noshoba offered.

"I hope so too, Noshoba. But ultimately, I want her to be happy. I hope I am the man for the job, but I will not stand in her way. I could not, anyway; she is pretty headstrong!"

Oh'Dar stooped over to put the brushes away,

straightening up just in time to take a direct blow to the face.

His one hand went instinctively to the pain, the other clenched in a fist. Pajackok did not give him time to recover, throwing another blow in his direction. Oh'Dar ducked just in time as Pajackok's fist went whizzing by.

He circled his opponent, looking for an opening. In the background, he could see Noshoba running as fast as he could to find Is'Taqa.

The opponents locked gazes. "What is your problem, Pajackok. Acise is right—it is her choice, not ours. Fighting will not solve anything."

"Maybe not, but it will make me feel better to beat you into the ground,"

"Not going to happen. We have known each other for a long time, all our lives, really. Is this what you want?"

"I had my eye on Acise from the time I was a young boy, Oh'Dar."

"Well, apparently she did not have hers on you, or she would not be so confused now and would have made that clear last night. I did not see her fighting for you when Honovi vacated your promise."

Pajackok roared and took another swing, but his elevated anger was putting him at a disadvantage. And the more Oh'Dar talked, the more contorted Pajackok's face became.

"Well, she did not choose you either, *White Man*," Pajackok said, throwing a serious insult.

"That is because I left her before. That was my mistake. One I will not make again. I thought I was doing the right thing, giving her time to think—instead, I only made her think I did not want her. I did, but I wanted more what was best for her."

"If you still wanted that, you would have left last night," Pajackok sneered.

"Again, it is *her* choice. If I am the one who lives in her heart, leaving will not change that."

Pajackok took a swing at Oh'Dar, who ducked in time and leaped forward and tackled the brave to the ground. He pinned Pajackok in place, using his height and greater weight as his father had taught him in hand-to-hand combat.

He could hear footsteps running toward them and realized that Noshoba must have found Is'Taqa.

"I thought I told you two to stop this," the Second Chief shouted as he pulled on Oh'Dar to get him to stand up.

Noshoba blurted out, "Pajackok started it! He came up and just hit Oh'Dar."

"Is that true, Pajackok?"

The brave looked away.

"You are disgracing your family. Attacking Oh'Dar will not make Acise choose you. If you do anything like this again, I will pay a visit to your father."

Pajackok held up both his palms toward Is'Taqa and backed away.

"Are you alright, Oh'Dar?"

Oh'Dar rubbed his jaw. "He landed a pretty good blow before I could defend myself. But I will live."

Oh'Dar shook his head to clear it, then asked, "What do you need help with today, Is'Taqa? I need to do something physical. The more taxing, the better."

The two men walked off together, with Noshoba in tow, Oh'Dar wondering, *If she does choose me, will Pajackok accept it?*

CHAPTER 5

It was almost a week since Oh'Dar had left. It was not that Acaraho expected him to have won Acise and returned this soon, but he did wonder what was going on. The new moon had passed, and each day brought them closer to the next full moon—when Haan had said his people would open Kthama Minor.

We still do not even know where it is; Adia would have told me if she had found out from Lifrin. It is so hard to accept all this, yet I have to. I experienced a taste of these mysterious areas in which the Healers work when Adia made the Connection with me so long ago. I still have not told her my side of the story—of how Lifrin saved both my life and Khon'Tor's. I do not know if it would help her to hear it now, or later, or if it even matters when.

Acaraho's crew had been working in one of the lowest levels of Kthama. An earthquake had weakened one of the tunnels. It was not commonly used, but any change in the structure of the corridors ran the chance of affecting the levels above.

Irka was working to determine the weak point in the tunnel when a load of rocks came loose and crushed him. He was obviously in terrible pain and just as obviously was not going to survive his wounds. Khon'Tor had sent back for Lifrin, letting her know the situation. While Lifrin administered to Irka, Acaraho and Khon'Tor supported the posts that had been put in place to shore up the rest of the tunnel.

Lifrin was crouched over Irka. She was soothing him with her words and touch, waiting for what she had given him to take effect. She could see that Khon'Tor was right. There was no way Irka could survive, even if they could extract him from the rubble that buried most of his body. Acaraho and Khon'Tor were both weakening from the extended period of holding the weight above them. There were none stronger than they were, nor would Acaraho agree to put another of his guards in danger. Acaraho knew Irka well, knew his mate and his offspring. His heart was heavy, knowing he would have to tell them that there had been an accident, and Irka had crossed over.

Suddenly, Lifrin shouted out, her arms waving wildly. "Get out, get out! Now! It is going to come down!" Acaraho started to reach for her, but as he moved his hand, the weight of the rock overhead shifted, and he had to put it back in place. "No, there is no time—leave me, please. If you do not, you will all die with me, and my death will have been for nothing!" she screamed.

Khon'Tor grabbed Acaraho and half dragged, half threw him out of the way just as the roof over Lifrin and where they had been standing, came crumbling down with a roar. Dust filled the air, covering everything. The two males coughed and stumbled up the corridor, trying to escape the billowing cloud that followed them.

Finally, far enough away, Acaraho and Khon'Tor stood, stunned. It had all happened so fast. They knew without a doubt Lifrin was gone, as of course was Irka.

"Her warning saved us both," said Acaraho, wiping the coating of dust from his face. "She has a younger brother, named Tar. We will need to provide for him. As far as I know, she is all the family he had," Acaraho said reverently, now staring at the rubble which had just become Lifrin's grave.

Khon'Tor brushed dust, dirt, and small pieces of rock off of himself. "It is a terrible loss, to lose one so young. And also a blow to High Rocks. We could both have been killed, Acaraho. No more working together on dangerous jobs like this. And see to it that Tar gets whatever he needs."

As soon as he could, Acaraho went to speak with Tar and held the young boy while he cried.

He had taken one of the older females with him. "This is Sarel. She will take care of you as long as you need her, and I will make sure that you are both provided for. It is not enough, but it is all I can do."

"Can I see her?" little Tar asked, breaking Acaraho's heart. He crouched back down to Tar's height, placing his hands on the youngster's shoulders. "No, Tar. You cannot. I am very sorry. But she gave her life for ours; she is a hero, never forget that."

He turned to look up at Sarel, "Come and see me later, please. I will have food sent here. I think it would be better for him to stay in his family quarters than move to yours if you do not mind."

"Yes, I agree. I would like to keep my own quarters as well, though, Commander, if that is permissible. When he is older, he will no doubt pair, and I would like to go back there. I will move some of my things over during the next few days."

Acaraho was pleased that Sarel had accepted when he asked her to take on Tar. She was a kind-hearted, loving female, mature, with patience and wisdom. Her offspring were grown and were out on their own. She could not replace Tar's sister, but she would gladly mother him as much as he would let her.

Over the years, Sarel made good her promise. She did everything she could to bond with Tar, yet he remained distant. It was if he had shut off that part of his heart forever, closing the door that would let another in. His needs were cared for, but he never let Sarel become more important to him that he could bear to lose.

When he was old enough, he told Sarel and Acaraho that he could make it on his own, and Sarel had moved back to her quarters. Though they kept in touch, Sarel never felt she had been able to help him heal, so impenetrable were the walls he built around himself—as impenetrable as the immovable pile of rock under which his sister's body remained.

Later that evening, when Adia and Acaraho retired, he told her the story of Tar. She listened quietly in his embrace, vowing again to fulfill Lifrin's dream that her brother would somehow find happiness in this lifetime.

That next day, Adia was still trying to catch up with Khon'Tor and Tehya. They had not come to the evening meal the day before. Now they were not at the first meal either, and neither was Tar, who was fresh on her mind after what Acaraho had shared last night.

As she sat finishing her food, the room seemed to tilt. She lost her balance and grabbed the edge of the table to keep from falling over.

I was dizzy before when I was carrying Nootau and

Nimida, but this feels different. Besides, am I far enough along to start feeling any side-effects?

Mapiya came out from behind the food preparation area and walked across, "Are you alright? Do you want me to find Acaraho?"

Adia put her hand to her forehead, "No, it will pass, I am sure." Before she sat down next to the Healer, Mapiya signed to one of the other females behind the counter to find Nadiwani or someone else to help Adia.

Khon'Tor and Tehya approached as Mapiya put an arm around Adia to steady her. "What is wrong, Adia?" asked Tehya.

Adia looked up and then returned to her position with her hand on her forehead. "Just dizzy, that is all."

To her relief, the feelings coming off both Khon'Tor and Tehya were more subdued now, calmer.

"Do you know how Haan's preparations are coming on?" she asked, not looking up.

"The place they prepared near Kayerm was destroyed. We found them a new place in the deer meadow up top. They are almost done preparing it," said Khon'Tor.

"That means they could start before too long," and she swayed slightly.

"Adia, are you alright? Is this because of what is about to happen? Or is it something else?"

"I do not know, Khon'Tor. We were not going to

say anything yet, but I am seeded, so it could be that."

"That is wonderful news," Mapiya congratulated her. "Acaraho must be so thrilled."

"Yes, he is; we both are. But the timing could have been better," Adia added.

"Congratulations. Do you want to keep it a secret?" Tehya asked.

"No. It just worked out that way with everything else going on."

"So, this will be his second offspring," Tehya exclaimed, thinking of Nootau.

Adia closed her eyes, not even wanting to acknowledge Tehya's statement. *What can I say, if I agree I am lying—*

"Let me get you some ginger water, that will help settle your stomach," offered Mapiya. As she got up to leave, Acaraho came walking briskly toward the table.

"Do you want to go to our quarters?" he asked, immediately noticing Adia's unsteadiness.

Without waiting for an answer, he scooped her up. As he carried her out of the Great Chamber, he said, "If any of you see Nadiwani, would you please send her our way?"

Adia nestled up against Acaraho, wrapping her arms around his neck. His chest was warm against her face. She wished she could stay in his arms forever, protected, safe. The strong rhythm of his stride was comforting, almost lulling her into sleep.

He shoved the door open with one shoulder and carried her to their sleeping mat. Once he had Adia comfortably placed on the bed, he turned back to take the ginger water from Mapiya, who had followed behind.

"I will check in on you later," Mapiya promised and left them to each other.

Acaraho smoothed the hair back from Adia's forehead and put an arm behind her back to prop her up. "Here, drink this,"

Adia took the gourd in both hands and sipped.

"More," he said.

She drank again and then shook her head, so he let her lay back down.

"Is it the offspring? Or something else?"

"I cannot tell. But it is powerful. I was sick with Nootau and Nimida, but it did not feel like this. This is—different. It feels as if the world is shifting out from under me. That is the only way I can explain it."

"Haan's people are done with their preparations. Perhaps something else they are doing is affecting you? I do not know what is involved."

"I wonder if Haaka knows anything about the ritual."

"Would you like me to bring her to you?"

Adia rolled over and curled into a ball and began rocking slowly back and forth. "I do not know; I do not know."

Acaraho could see she was miserable. He soothed

her hair away from her forehead and rested his other hand on her hip.

"You and Urilla Wuti seem to be in this together, I wonder if she is feeling it?" he said out loud. "I am going to check on her. I will be back as soon as I can."

He sat the unfinished ginger water down within reach and covered her up before he left.

Acaraho announced himself at Urilla Wuti's quarters. As he was about to give up, she opened the door.

"Yes, Commander?"

"Adia is not well. I do not know if it is being seeded or something else. Are you experiencing any discomfort?"

"Take me to her," said Urilla Wuti, and then she stumbled.

"Are you alright? I know you feel it is improper, but if you have to see Adia, may I carry you? You appear too weak to walk that far."

It was improper, but with great reluctance, Urilla Wuti relented. "Yes, I need to see her, so in this case, I will permit it,"

Acaraho gently lifted her and carried her to his quarters. He set her down on the mat next to Adia, who turned over with a surprised look on her face.

"Urilla Wuti," she said and curled back up into a ball. "Everything is off. It is like the world has shifted off-center. I cannot get grounded."

"I am experiencing the same thing. I was able to mitigate it by opening the Corridor, though not entering. Try it yourself."

Adia became very silent and still. Acaraho could not tell if anything was happening, but he noticed that Adia's body seemed to release some of its tension.

After a moment, Adia turned partially toward Urilla Wuti.

"That helped. What do you think it is?"

"It must be something to do with what Haan's people are up to."

Adia glanced up at her mate, not wanting to alarm him but needing to talk to Urilla Wuti.

"Acaraho, I am fine; you can leave us."

"No. Whatever you are going to say, I want to hear it."

That is the last thing I want, to worry him more than he already is. But I need to talk to Urilla Wuti. So, Adia went ahead and asked the older Healer, "Do you think that entering the Corridor is a means of protection for us, for what is to come?"

"It seemed to work in this case. But I have the impression that we need to be present for what is about to happen. That whatever energy will be released is something we must experience. I am sure if remaining in the Corridor was an option, Lifrin would have told us."

"You are talking about her as if she is still alive," Acaraho interjected.

"She is, Acaraho," Adia explained. "Everyone is. Everyone who has crossed over is still alive in the Great Spirit. I almost said that they are alive somewhere, but there is no concept of time and space in the Corridor; it only appears so because that is how we expect the world to be."

"I am frustrated with this. How am I to keep you safe when we do not know what we are dealing with or what is about to happen," said Acaraho. Then he narrowed his eyes. "We need answers from Haan. I am going to get him—now," and he stormed off.

Acaraho made his way up to the meadow. The sun was still in the east, and dew was still sparkling on the leaves and branches of the perimeter. The meadow was eerily silent; only the slightest breeze could be heard rustling the treetops.

Haan's people had placed massive stones in a circle, and the rays of sunlight made flecks within the granite sparkle with a magical quality. At first, Acaraho did not see Haan or anyone. He looked around again and finally saw something.

The Sarnonn were nearly invisible, one standing in front of each of the huge grey boulders. Twelve stones were arranged in a circle, and they had clearly been dug partially into the ground. It was nearly impossible to see the Sarnonn because they seemed to disappear and blend into the stones behind them. They were standing with their arms to their sides, unmoving. Acaraho looked around the circle; each of them was positioned the same. There was no movement, and though their eyes were open, there was no acknowledgment that they had seen him. Acaraho shuddered. Behind the stones was a ring of the rest of the Sarnonn, also standing straight and unmoving.

Whatever this is, it looks like it has started. Great Spirit, help us all.

Acaraho felt as if he was imposing, that he had entered a sacred area where he did not belong. He wondered what protected them in this state, and then decided perhaps the state itself did.

I have no idea what to expect. Whatever is going to happen, we are not prepared, and I do not like that at all. I need to find Khon'Tor and let him know about this.

Acaraho found his First Guard, Awan.

"Assemble everyone you can—watchers, whoever you can spare, anyone who is not on guard duty outside Kthama. Something is about to happen. I need them all here as soon as possible. Where is Khon'Tor?"

"I believe he is with his mate in the Great Chamber."

Acaraho slapped Awan on the shoulder and left.

He found Khon'Tor and Tehya sitting together with Nadiwani, Nimida, Nootau, and Tar, whom Nimida had coaxed back into joining the group. "Khon'Tor, a word?"

The Leader got up from the bench and stepped away with Acaraho.

"Something is happening, Khon'Tor. You saw how sick Adia was. Well, Urilla Wuti is feeling it too; she is with Adia in our quarters. I went up to the meadow above to find Haan. I found him and twelve of his followers. They were standing like statues in front of those huge stones they placed in a circle up there. Not moving, eyes open but not blinking. The rest were standing in an outer circle with the same blank look on their faces. I do not think they even saw me there."

"So, it has started, whatever *it* is," said Khon'Tor.

"I do not know how to protect us from this. I do not know what this even is. And on top of everything else, I am worried sick about Adia." Acaraho put his hand to his head.

Khon'Tor stared at him. In all his years, he had seldom seen Acaraho like this. But then Acaraho, like him, now had something to lose—something irreplaceable. Adia's being seeded just added to it. "Adia told us this morning that she is with offspring," he said.

Acaraho nodded. "I am sure that whatever Haan is involved in is making them both sick. And if it has just started, how much worse will it get before it is over?" He was nearly beside himself now.

Tehya was watching from the table. Seeing the High Commander in such distress, she got up and went over to him. She put her hand out and touched Acaraho's arm and looked up at him softly.

"Adia is strong, Acaraho. She is called to this. They both are. And she is not facing this alone; she has you to fight for her, with her. There are no mistakes; I truly believe this."

Acaraho stopped a moment at what Tehya had just said. "Everything I know about fighting—about protecting those I am responsible for—none of my skills will help here. This is altogether different. This is not a physical fight; it is a spiritual one." Then he paused before continuing. "Khon'Tor, I think I know what we need to do."

"What is it, Commander? Anything—"

"Pray."

Khon'Tor blinked.

"We need everyone in the community to come together and pray. Adia told me a little bit about what she and Urilla Wuti were working on. It has to do with strengthening boundaries. We need a different kind of protection now. One that will take all of us to provide."

"I will call an assembly. Give a few minutes for everyone to come."

"I am going to speak with my charges, and then I will be there."

Acaraho returned to the Great Entrance, where Awan had assembled a large number of guards and watchers as requested. They turned to him as he approached.

"Thank you for coming. I am grateful to each one of you. I know that you are dedicated, loyal, and skilled in all forms of combat. Those of you who are watchers, your senses are keen, sharp, focused. Guards, you are physically at your peak—ready at any moment to defend Kthama with your lives if necessary. We are about to be impacted by something which few of those abilities, as great as they are, will protect our people."

They looked at each other in confusion.

"You know that we have made contact with the Sarnonn, and you know that their Leader, Haan, has brought a band of followers with him, with the intention of opening Kthama Minor. We do not know what Kthama Minor is, other than that it is some lost portion of Kthama. We do not know where the entrance is located. Nor do we know what will happen when it is opened. From what I have heard, there will be a release of energy that could affect all of us."

"Energy? Forgive me, Commander, but what are you talking about?" one of his guards asked.

"The magnetic currents, you know how to sense them. It is similar. Have you not ever walked into a room and immediately noticed the tension? Or entered a meadow and felt the peace and sanctity of it? That is energy. The flow of the magnetic currents we feel—that help us navigate our lands—that is energy too. We do not really speak of it in such a way; it is usually only spoken of in the Healers' realm. But now we do need to speak of it. We need to focus our efforts spiritually. For Kthama, for everyone we love and hold dear."

"Are you asking us to pray?"

"Yes. Basically, yes. Khon'Tor is calling an assembly about it."

"We can do that, Commander."

Acaraho sighed. "Come to the Great Chamber when you hear the Call To Assembly Horn."

Meanwhile, Khon'Tor had gone to Acaraho's quarters in search of Urilla Wuti and Adia.

They both looked up when he entered. It was immediately clear to Khon'Tor how sick they were.

"Acaraho went up to the meadow. Something is happening. Haan and his followers are standing in front of the stones they set in the ground. They are not moving or speaking. I am calling everyone together, and I need you both to come."

Adia and Urilla Wuti looked at each other.

"I know you are not feeling well. But we need your direction. Tell the People what to do. There must be something. Even after the ravages of the sickness, we are still many. A collective effort may help."

"He is right, Adia. We are not thinking clearly. This is not a physical battle—this is a spiritual one. We can direct the People to focus their attention on protecting all of us. It is the best chance we have."

"We will need help to get there."

"I will come back with Acaraho. We will manage," he said.

For the second time ever, Urilla Wuti allowed herself to be carried, this time in Khon'Tor's arms. Acaraho brought Adia. When they had sat them down on the platform, Khon'Tor gave the signal for the Call To Assembly Horn to be blown.

Within a few minutes, people were streaming into the Great Chamber from all directions. There had been no advance notice of a meeting, which meant the urgency was great. It did not take long for the People to settle in.

Tehya sat next to Adia and Urilla Wuti at the front, rubbing first Adia's back and then Urilla Wuti's. Seated with the crowd, Mapiya held Arismae. Haaka stood at the back with Kalli.

"Thank you for coming. As I explained the last time we gathered, the Sarnonn have brought to us much lost knowledge about our past, including the lost cave system of Kthama Minor. And that after preparations were made, Kthama Minor would be opened by the Sarnonn. That time is at hand."

Khon'Tor looked over at Urilla Wuti and Adia, seeing if they were in any shape at all to speak. Tehya shook her head no.

"We all know that life does not consist only of the physical world of Etera and that there are other powers at work in the spiritual realm. In this same vein, the opening of Kthama Minor is not just a physical act.

There are also changes being enacted at other levels." Khon'Tor motioned toward the two Healers. "As you can see, both of the Healers are struggling, and it is connected to what I am about to ask you to do. What looks like a physical illness affecting them, is a challenge from another plane—somewhere beyond Etera."

Those present looked at each other in concern.

"The High Protector and First Guard Awan are committed to thwarting any physical attack, though we have no natural enemies. The watchers survey our land, telling the hunters when the migrations have begun, which resources are abundant in the area, and which are challenged. They monitor the skies, giving us warning of any impending rough weather. They also help our Brothers since we have watchers placed on their territory, too. But the concerns we are facing today are not on this level. They are not on a level that can be seen, heard, touched, or smelled. They are on the level that most of us never encounter—the seventh realm of the Healers."

"But though we do not work in that realm and know little of it, that does not mean we cannot help. Collectively we are physically strong. I believe that we are also collectively spiritually strong. Unfortunately, I do not have the knowledge to instruct you about how we can help. I need Adia and Urilla Wuti to direct you."

He turned to look at them. Tehya was trying to help Adia to her feet but was too small to be of much help. Acaraho came over and sat behind her instead, letting her brace herself against him so she could address the crowd.

"We do not know how Haan's people are going to open Kthama Minor, but we believe that, however it is to be done, they have started," said Adia. "And Urilla Wuti and I are feeling the effects. What Khon'Tor is asking, what I am asking, is that over the upcoming days, you devote as much time as you can to prayer."

"What are we praying for?" asked someone.

"I say *prayer*, but it is a little different. You know how, when you look forward to something, you can visualize it in your mind? You picture your offspring's first steps, the first fresh taste of the black summer berries, the warm sun on your face? I need you all to picture a wall. A gigantic wall with a roof, all around Kthama, protecting it and all of us here. A shimmering, vibrant, beautiful bubble of energy."

"What is it made of, Healer? What should we picture it made of?"

"Love, Pakuna," answered Adia. "Picture it as a ball of love—impenetrable, powerful, encasing all of us in the protection and care of the Great Spirit. Do not worry about getting it exactly right. Your intention of protection for us all will be enough."

"Is this dangerous? What is about to happen?" another voice shouted out.

"I believe that we may all be affected by it, you may experience dizziness, a sense of things being off

—I do not know. The greatest impact will be to those of us who are Healers—Urilla Wuti, perhaps Nadiwani, and myself." Adia answered.

The faces staring back at Adia looked concerned, worried. Frightened.

As low as possible, Adia whispered to Urilla Wuti, *"We should have thought of this earlier, started this earlier. Khon'Tor's announcement that this would be coming was not enough. How do I soothe them?"*

To which Urilla Wuti whispered, *"Look at their faces, Adia. They are afraid. Fear and faith cannot exist in the same soul at once."*

Suddenly, Urilla Wuti spoke, "Do not be concerned, People of the High Rocks. Your participation will be of real benefit to us and help ease us through this transition. But we will be fine, regardless. As Adia said, however often you can join with us in this will be greatly appreciated. There is no power greater than that of love. And there is no greater love than that which you have for each other, this I have seen for myself."

Khon'Tor stepped forward and took back the floor, raising his hand to speak. "We are powerful because our concern and care for each other are powerful. The help we need from you is not on the physical plane. I cannot tell you what will happen in the next few hours or days. Just as the rolling thunder can be alarming, but is truly harmless, whatever it is, even if it seems disturbing, remember we have no reason to believe it is dangerous. It is only that forces are shifting on another plane—forces that we believe will ultimately benefit us in the long run. Please make what the Healers have asked a priority over the next few days. Thank you for coming. That is all," and he dropped his hand and turned his attention to Tehya and the Healers.

Acaraho stepped forward. "We need to get them back to where they can rest—" he stopped midsentence, looking up.

Pieces of dirt, small rocks, and debris were raining down from the ceiling above the Great Chamber. A rhythmic thump was echoing down through the layers of rock above, even though it was from some distance away.

Someone, or something—something *powerful*—was on the move in the meadow above Kthama.

CHAPTER 6

Acaraho reached down and scooped up Adia. "I am taking you back to our quarters," he said.

"No. I have to know what is going on. Something miraculous is happening, and we need to go outside. It will not matter where I am, Acaraho. Whatever is happening will still affect us. I need to know, and so does Urilla Wuti."

Khon'Tor stood where he was and again addressed the murmuring crowd. Their faces were turned up to the ceiling in alarm.

"Return to your quarters. Set aside your fear and do as the Healers have instructed. Kthama has stood for thousands of years; she will stand for thousands more."

Khon'Tor, Acaraho, Urilla Wuti, Adia, Nadiwani, and several of the guards left Kthama to investigate. The sound of the thumping was much louder outside. They could tell it was coming from the direction of the Sarnonn's meadow.

They arrived in time to see a wall of dark-haired bodies coming down the path from above. A giant wall of strength that seemed to move as one body. Each step was in unison, the same stride, the same cadence. This was what had shaken the meadow above. Each set of Sarnonn eyes was staring blankly; their attention was directed somewhere else, seeing but not seeing. Nearly thirty massive towering bodies were moving as one, but under what direction and to where?

As they came around the bend at the bottom of the path, Khon'Tor could see Haan in the lead. All the eyes of the Sarnonn were vacant, except for Haan's. The Sarnonn Leader looked at Khon'Tor as he approached.

"We are Sarnonn. We are here to create the future of our making. Stay back lest you be trampled, or join us on our way to what is to be," and he looked again in the direction he was headed.

The others were standing behind their Leader, watching. Somehow the Sarnonn had become one mind with one purpose. Acaraho shuddered, thinking what damage they could do under that control. Each synchronized step made the ground shake under the impact of their weight, and as they were walking in single file, it took a while for the Sarnonn to pass.

The People's Leaders watched them file past.

Acaraho was supporting Adia, and First Guard Awan had his arm around Urilla Wuti.

"Where are they going?" wondered Khon'Tor aloud. No one answered because there was no answer to give.

Once the last Sarnonn had passed, Khon'Tor and the others followed. As they walked, Khon'Tor had a sinking feeling about the path they were on. It was off-limits and was not directly connected with the others. Most of the paths wound around and afforded short cuts that led to others, but this one was avoided. In fact, the only time Khon'Tor could think of anyone on this path it was either Nadiwani —or *Adia*.

Khon'Tor stopped, almost causing the others to bump into him.

"What is it?" asked Acaraho, carrying Adia directly behind him.

Khon'Tor looked at Adia, "This is—"

"Yes, Khon'Tor," she said quietly. It was the path on which Khon'Tor had attacked and violated her so many years ago. She had barely traveled it since that time.

Up ahead, Haan swept his powerful arms to rip away the overgrown brush that now covered the narrowing path. He picked up and easily tossed away fallen tree branches that blocked their progress. He followed the path around. Finally, the Sarnonn stopped. They had reached their destination. They stood silently—as if waiting for the Akassa behind them to catch up.

When Khon'Tor and his band made it through the brush, they found themselves looking at the backs of nearly thirty twelve-foot giants, aligned in a perfect semi-circle facing an insurmountable rock wall.

Adia and Nadiwani turned to each other. Khon'Tor looked up to see what the point of the Sarnonn's focus could be. All he saw was a giant rock wall perhaps sixty, eighty feet high, covered in thick woody vines. There looked to be a huge boulder, partially protruding from the back wall and covered by ages' worth of dirt and overgrowth.

"Where are we?" Khon'Tor asked. "What are they staring at?"

"The Healers' Stone," said Adia. "This is the Healer's Cove. A sacred place for the Healers of the High Rocks for generations. Back to the days of the Ancients."

Haan and his Healer Artadel turned to face each other. Each extended his arms horizontally, and they pressed their palms together. Then they raised their hands overhead, palms still touching. Suddenly, the mass of Sarnonn started moving. They formed a circle around Haan and Artadel and simultaneously began walking in a clockwise direction.

Then all together, they started chanting.

Just as the chanting was becoming uncomfort-ably loud, it stopped abruptly, and the circle broke formation. As one, the group moved silently forward and lined up, each Sarnonn placing their palms flat against the face of the giant rock. In unison, the Sarnonn started chanting again.

Adia and Urilla Wuti started swaying. Acaraho increased his support of Adia, just as Awan did the same for Urilla Wuti.

None of them could understand quite what the Sarnonn were saying.

"An ancient language, older than either of ours," said Nadiwani—the only one of the females seemingly unaffected.

"What are they saying? I wish we knew." Khon'Tor was standing back at a safe distance.

"We are Mothoc," Adia said.

Everyone immediately turned to face her.

"We are Mothoc. We are Legion. The Age of Shadows is at hand. The true test has begun. We will be watching."

Acaraho looked over at his mate, who seemed to be in some type of altered state. As the Sarnonn continued to chant, Adia chanted with them in the unknown language, occasionally stopping to repeat it in the words of the People, "We are Mothoc. We are Legion. The Age of Shadows is at hand. The true test has begun. We will be watching."

As the Sarnonn voices grew louder, a slow rumbling started. Pieces of dirt, stones, and twigs dislodged from the great stone and came tumbling down. The sound of rock breaking and cracking became the backdrop to the deep Sarnonn voices still chanting in unison.

Slowly, Haan and Artadel began turning with their upraised palms still pressed together, their gazes locked. As they turned, the creaking and snapping sounds became louder. Dark clouds formed as if from nowhere, turning twilight to night. The wind increased, throwing more debris across the alcove.

As more and more soil and accumulation fell from the face of the great rock, the others could make out a symbol, one carved long ago, up toward the top. They stared at it, an ancient marker hidden by the passage of time and the thick overgrowth of vines.

The spectators were driven to take a step back, but not by any earthly pressure. It was as if a gale-force wind was making it difficult for them to stand. As if something was about to break free. They could now all feel it, every one of them dizzy and overwhelmed.

Khon'Tor felt behind him for Tehya, and finding her hand, pulled her in front of him. He wrapped his arms around her to keep her safe, partially turning so they could both still see. At the back, Haaka watched in awe, shielding Kalli protectively.

Suddenly, Haan and the other Sarnonn stopped turning. The chanting stopped. Acaraho looked at Adia again; she seemed still to be in some type of trance.

Haan and the other Sarnonn pulled their hands

apart. And then with a resounding clap, slammed their palms together again. At the moment of impact, every one of the vacant-eyed Sarnonn shouted, "Wrak-Ayya."

All of Khon'Tor's people gasped.

There was a clap of rolling thunder, and a blinding shaft of light shot straight up from the meadow above. At that exact moment, Adia cried out and curled into a ball, grabbing her belly, then both she and Urilla Wuti lost consciousness, falling limp into the arms of Acaraho and Awan.

Rivers of molten light began to stream up both sides of the giant stone and along the edges to meet at the top. A small crack formed around its embedded curve and grew larger as some unseen power began to force the rock out of position. Finally, with a resounding crack, the giant barrier to the entrance of Kthama Minor broke free.

Every one of the People watching reached up to cover their ears, protecting them from the deafening sound of the massive rock scraping along the ground. The same blinding light streaking skyward from the meadow above now spilled out from around the edges of the massive stone.

As if on cue, the Sarnonn simultaneously moved backward out of the way, watching the rock move toward them.

Acaraho set Adia down on the ground in a safer spot and signaled for Awan to bring Urilla Wuti. He motioned, and a circle of guards came over. "Stand here around them. Make sure nothing harms them," he yelled as he crouched at Adia's side.

Suddenly, the rock stopped moving. It had been pushed out by some unimaginable power, perhaps twenty feet from its original position.

Nobody moved. Everything became deathly silent. It was not over yet.

In the next moment, with no notice, the Sarnonn were moving again. Two of them filed in and disappeared behind the great rock. Haan and the others remained outside. Once again, there was a sound of stone scraping against the hard ground. Khon'Tor led Tehya over to the protected custody of the guards encircling Adia and Urilla Wuti, then stepped forward without her, heading past Haan and Artadel, both of whom paid him no notice. He moved around the giant rock and could see the Sarnonn working in unison to pull aside a boulder that was smaller though still impressive, forcing it to give up access to whatever chamber existed behind it.

When it had cleared the opening, the Sarnonn stepped back, and Khon'Tor had to move quickly to avoid being crushed or knocked down. They filed out and assumed a semi-circle around Haan and Artadel.

Once again, the two raised their palms, and each smacked his against those of the other.

In the next second, Haan declared, "Kah-Sol 'Rin."

The state of Ror'Eckrah was released, and every Sarnonn except Haan and Artadel collapsed and slipped to the ground. The wide beam of light shooting up into the darkened sky from the meadow above suddenly retracted and disappeared. The clouds which had earlier darkened the sky to inky blackness began to dissipate.

Acaraho watched it all unfold, still kneeling next to Adia and Urilla Wuti behind the protective circle of guards. The moment the Sarnonn collapsed, Adia and Urilla Wuti had both begun to regain consciousness.

Acaraho lifted Adia and pulled her close to him, his hands shaking with relief that she was alright.

"Where am I?" she asked, blinking and trying to open her eyes. "Where is Urilla Wuti?"

"She is right here. We are outside what you call the Healer's Cove. The Sarnonn just unsealed what is called Kthama Minor."

She put her hand to her head and closed her eyes. "Kah-Sol 'Rin," she said, repeating the words that Haan had just spoken. "It is done."

A million questions with no answers raced through Acaraho's mind, the only one that mattered being whether Adia would be alright. He helped her sit up and waited for her to get her bearings.

Adia glanced over at Urilla Wuti, who was being helped by Awan. The older Healer looked her way and nodded that she was unharmed.

Whatever cloud was covering Haan's consciousness cleared. The other Sarnonn started slowly coming to, looking around before standing. Haan shook his head and looked at Artadel. Then they both turned to see that the giant rock had been dislodged. They observed the light coming from within and knew the second rock had also been moved away.

"It is done, Adik'Tar," said Artadel. "Kthama Minor is open to the Akassa of the High Rocks."

Haan turned around and motioned for Khon'Tor to approach. The People's Leader was not sure what to say. "Thank you" seemed to be ludicrous, inappropriate, hardly sufficient. "Will your people recover?" he asked.

"Yes. However, they will need to return to the meadow to rejuvenate; both the males and the females."

In all the melee, Khon'Tor had never considered that some of them were females. "Is there anything we can do to help you? Can we bring you food, perhaps? Water?"

"There is the stream above for water. There is enough to eat; we prepared ahead of time," explained Haan.

"What will your people do now? Will they return to Kayerm? Will they stay; is there more for them to do?"

"I do not know, Khon'Tor. We have no place to go. Now that we have opened Kthama Minor, returning to Kayerm will only spark the civil war that is already smoldering. But we can stay in the meadow until we figure it out."

Khon'Tor felt more than a twinge of conscience. *They sacrificed everything to help us, and as a result, their people are bitterly divided. Hakani, Haan's mate, is dead; his adopted son of my blood, whom he raised, is missing and possibly also dead.*

Just then, Haaka emerged from the back, carrying Kalli. "Haan," and she rushed to him.

He put his arm around her and pulled her into a hug. Haaka looked up at him with a mixture of adoration and awe.

"Are you doing alright here?" Haan asked, his gaze including Kalli. "Yes. We are fine. They are very kind. In truth, Haan, it will be difficult to leave."

Haan nodded. He knew the fact that the Sarnonn had nowhere to go bothered her immensely.

"Haan, would you like to join Haaka in her quarters?" Khon'Tor asked, watching the exchange between the two Sarnonn.

"Thank you, but no. I need to stay with my followers. It would not be proper to leave them in the meadow while I enjoy the luxury of Kthama."

Again, a prick of conscience hit Khon'Tor. *I do not want them to live in Kthama. But how is this to be resolved? It is because they helped us that they are homeless.*

As if Haan had read Khon'Tor's mind, he said, "Do not trouble yourself over it, Khon'Tor. You are right. It is best they do not experience what it is like to live inside Kthama. It might prove too much of a temptation, even for these who are faithful to my leadership. The Akassa were fortunate to keep Kthama the first time."

That last statement was not lost on Khon'Tor or Acaraho.

Haan looked over at the entrance to Kthama Minor, now open. "Do you wish to enter?"

Khon'Tor glanced back at Tehya and the others; they looked exhausted. But the curiosity was overwhelming.

"I will go," he said and stepped forward.

It was massive, an immovable piece of granite. The forces that had placed it must have been enormous, and it had now shifted from its centuries-old position. *If I start thinking about what moved this rock—or who—I may not be able to continue.*

Behind the first was the second boulder.

This one, with enough of us together, we would have been able to move. But never the first one. Without the Sarnonn, there would have been no way to open Kthama Minor, even if we had known it existed and where to find it.

Khon'Tor's mind was reeling. It was too much to try to sort out just then. *Why create a Rah-hora forbidding the Sarnonn to contact us, yet leave the knowledge of Kthama Minor with the Healer of the People of the High*

Rocks, when we could never open it without the help of the Sarnonn. Something is missing—or am I simply too tired to follow it now?

Then he noticed a mark on the second rock, similar to the symbol on the first. "Haan," he called out.

Haan came forward and saw what Khon'Tor was looking up at.

"Wrak-Ayya," he said. "It is the symbol for Wrak-Ayya, the Age of Shadows."

"What was the one on the first rock?"

"Wrak-Wavara, the Age of Darkness."

So, this is how it begins. How could we have been so wrong? Was it really never the Waschini who posed a threat? Was it our own future? Or rather, the sins of our past returning to haunt us? By opening Kthama Minor, we have now entered the Age of Shadows. But what does that even mean? Shadows of what? The more we learn, the less we know.

Khon'Tor moved around the second rock to see a large, inner chamber, much like Kthama's Great Entrance. He was about to step foot inside the second entrance, but something stopped him. *No. This is too important a step for one person, even a Leader, to take alone.* "Haan, I will wait until the others are able to join me. I will send a messenger to you when we are ready."

Haan nodded and stepped outside again. He put his arm around Haaka and led her away from the opening. "Return to Kthama with our daughter; I will ask for you in a few days."

Haaka nodded, and as she walked away, she whispered Haan's words to herself, "*Our* daughter?"

Haan joined his followers, and they made their way back to the meadow.

Khon'Tor returned to the guards who still surrounded Acaraho, Nadiwani, Tehya, and the Healers. "We must enter together. When we are all able."

Awan gathered up Urilla Wuti, but Adia began to rise on her own. Once she was standing, Acaraho supported her with his arm and turned to the guards.

"Are you feeling any ill effects? Dizziness? Pain? Disorientation?" he asked them. "Very well then, remain here. Surround the opening but do *not* enter. If you feel you are in danger, leave your post and find safety. Otherwise, I will have you relieved when we return, well before morning."

Khon'Tor and the others turned back to Kthama. On the way, they made plans to meet before moonrise to enter Kthama Minor if the Healers were up to it by then.

Adia sat down on the mat in the Healer's Quarters, and Awan set Urilla Wuti down next to her. Nadiwani sat in front of them, looking them over. Also exhausted, Khon'Tor, Tehya, and the others found places to rest.

Khon'Tor waited for Nadiwani to finish examining the Healers. "Are you both alright? You were unconscious for a while. And during that time, the Sarnonn started chanting. We could not tell what they were saying, but you, Adia—you translated it for us. But it was as if you were not really you."

Adia and Urilla Wuti were silent, exhausted.

"What were they saying?" Khon'Tor asked.

Tehya spoke up, "I memorized it, *"We are Mothoc. We are Legion. The Age of Shadows is at hand. The true test has begun. We will be watching."*

"The odd use of the term we, as if spoken by the Mothoc, not the Sarnonn," said Nadiwani

"What we just witnessed was like nothing I have ever seen or heard of before," commented Khon'Tor. "It was as if every Sarnonn was under Haan's control. Each movement, each step they took was exactly the same as the others. Their eyes looked vacant—as if they were all seeing only through his eyes. But even Haan did not seem like himself."

Acaraho looked at both the Healers with concern. "Khon'Tor, they are exhausted. Perhaps we should let them rest."

"I will not take anyone in there without some discussion between us about what happened," Khon'Tor declared. "Now."

Also exhausted, Acaraho forced himself to keep the conversation moving as Khon'Tor had directed. "All we can say is that Kthama Minor has been opened. From there, we take it one step at a time.

Haan's people are back in the meadow; he said they could not go back to Kayerm," added Acaraho.

"I feel guilty about it. But I cannot let them into Kthama. Even Haan understands that. Somehow, we must help them find another place to stay."

"Kthama Minor," said Urilla Wuti.

"What?"

"They could move into Kthama Minor. That is if it is habitable after all these centuries."

Acaraho and Khon'Tor frowned at each other. Neither was sure they wanted to give away such a strategic location.

"We do not need to decide tonight," said Khon'-Tor. "Let us wait until we know more about Kthama Minor. Having them there would put them in direct proximity to Kthama."

Acaraho understood what Khon'Tor was saying. Just because there was goodwill between the two tribes did not mean there always would be. And there was the rebel group back at Kayerm.

"I understand, Khon'Tor," Acaraho said. "I am also hesitant. Perhaps after we inspect it and learn more about it. The advantage is that they would prevent the other faction of the Sarnonn from moving in. We know they *are* against us. As for Haan's followers and their proximity or lack of it, if they should turn against us, distance will not make any difference either way. They might be a powerful ally, considering the circumstances."

Acaraho was right. Khon'Tor ran his hand

through his hair, also suddenly realizing how tired he was.

Tehya stepped over and put her hand against his face. "Adoeete, perhaps we should all rest. We can meet again in several hours. That will still give us time to have a discussion before we enter Kthama Minor. And our minds will have a chance to work through some of this."

He reached up and smoothed her hand, looking lovingly into her eyes. He knew she must be concerned about Arismae. Then he realized what he was doing in front of the others, and quickly dropped his hand. "Awan, on your way back, would you check in with Mapiya and ask her to bring Arismae back to nurse and then keep her for the rest of the evening?"

Tehya leaned against him, her head pressed to his shoulder, and nodded her agreement.

"If it is acceptable, then, we will reconvene in my meeting room when you have rested. Thank you. That is all."

Acaraho turned to Urilla Wuti. "Would you prefer to stay here or go back to your quarters?"

Nadiwani volunteered, "If you would just as soon stay here, I will be glad to stay with you."

Urilla Wuti nodded and closed her eyes.

Awan said he would come around and fetch them later, so they need not worry about oversleeping. In the meantime, he would line up other guards to replace those remaining at Kthama Minor.

Acaraho scooped Adia up and carried her back to

their quarters. He laid her on the sleeping mat, covered her up, and she was asleep within moments. He lay watching her for some time, thanking the Great Spirit that she had come through this alright. Or, at least for now, that she seemed to have.

Tehya was sound asleep almost the moment she had finished nursing Arismae and made herself comfortable on the mat in the Leader's Quarters. Khon'Tor stretched out behind his mate and encased her with his large muscular frame. He pulled the cover up and wrapped an arm around her. Deep, steady breathing told him she was sleeping. He fell asleep shortly after, but not before saying a prayer that Tehya would not have another of her nightmares.

It seemed only moments before it was time to get up and meet. Khon'Tor wished Tehya would stay in their quarters and rest some more, but she insisted on joining him and the others. "I am your mate— Third Rank. My place is with you," she insisted.

They were not the first to the meeting room. Everyone but Urilla Wuti was there. Noticing her absence, Khon'Tor was immediately alarmed.

"Where is Urilla Wuti?" he asked.

"She is in the Healer's Quarters with Nadiwani. She was not up to coming; that is all."

Khon'Tor looked around the rest of the circle.

Acaraho, Adia, Awan, Tehya. Oh'Dar. "Where is Oh'Dar?" he asked, realizing he had not seen the young male for a while, not since gifting them with the giant seating construction.

"He is with the Brothers. Winning back Acise, I hope," said Acaraho.

Khon'Tor sat silent for a moment. "When will he return?"

"We do not know. I told him not to come back without winning her heart," Acaraho told the Leader with a faint grin.

"Well, Commander, hopefully, it will not take him as long to win her as it took you to win Adia. Otherwise, he will be gone a while."

"I am anxious to enter Kthama Minor. But I am also wary," said Acaraho, changing the subject. "It is illogical to think there is anything in there waiting to harm us, I know. In the opening of the entrance, alone, we have seen evidence of forces beyond our understanding. If whatever it is behind this wanted to harm us, they could certainly have accomplished it before now. Something or someone wants us to have access to whatever secrets Kthama Minor holds."

Awan nodded. "I agree with the High Protector. I do not believe there is a real basis for our fears. That is not to say that whatever we find will not affect us. There is also the possibility that, once inside, the Healers will experience additional effects."

"I have questions," said Khon'Tor. "It seems all I

have lately are questions. Why create a Rah-hora banning the Sarnonn from having contact with us, but then pass down knowledge of Kthama Minor through the Healers of the High Rocks—when only the Sarnonn had the power to open it back up? It does not make sense."

"Perhaps the answers are inside," suggested Adia. "It appears we are on a path, a trajectory. All we can do is continue to walk down the way that is being laid out for us. I agree, Khon'Tor—if whoever placed that rock and sealed Kthama Minor did not want us ever to re-enter it, then why pass on knowledge of it and make a way for it to be opened? There are supernatural forces involved here."

"How do you feel, Adia?" asked Tehya.

"I am still a little dizzy. As if something in the world has shifted—is out of phase. But it is not as strong as it was earlier."

"*We are Mothoc. We are Legion. The Age of Shadows is at hand. The true test has begun. We will be watching.* That is what you told us they were saying, Adia—when they were chanting together before the stone was slid out of place. Have you heard any of this before?" Khon'Tor asked.

"The Healer's Cove has always been a place of refuge and reflection for the High Rocks Healers. I have sat and looked at that rock so many times. I have wondered how it got there, as it did not appear to be a natural part of the rest of the wall. I often felt the significance of the place—there was a feeling of mystery about it—but I assumed that all the Healers before me also did. I sometimes had a feeling that there were secrets there from ages past, but I cannot explain what is going on, Khon'Tor. Somehow, I knew what they were saying. If we take it literally, and I would hesitate to take it any other way, then they were channeling something. They did not say W*e are Sarnonn*. They said W*e are Mothoc*. Can it be possible that the Mothoc survived, and from a distance have the power to affect the Sarnonn so powerfully?"

"It has certainly deeply affected you and Urilla Wuti," Khon'Tor said.

"It was like being a step out of place. As if Etera had shifted off-center. I phased in and out. Sometimes I was one of the Sarnonn; at other times, I was nowhere. A powerful feeling of agelessness, or something older than time, passed through me—something wanting to be known, waiting for us to come after all this time. I do not have the words to explain it. I have not had a chance to talk to Urilla Wuti, but I believe she experienced the same," Adia explained.

"We have to suspend our natural dependency on what we think we know," Khon'Tor mused. "It was not long ago that we had any idea the Sarnonn still existed—let alone so close to our community. We believed the Sarnonn somehow bred with the Brothers, but now we know that is not true. We know that they are more our cousins than our ancestors. Just as we have learned that our history is wrong, so we must let go of what we thought was fact. We must take this one step at a time and try to open our minds to possibilities we may find—incomprehensible."

Around the room, heads nodded.

"Are we ready?" asked Acaraho.

More nodding.

"In which case, I will send a messenger for Haan."

"We are on our way," said Khon'Tor, rising from his seat.

They headed out of Kthama, Acaraho stopping on the way to collect the guards Awan had lined up to relieve those still at the Healer's Cove, and to send a messenger for Haan.

With each step closer, they felt their anxiety rise. But with the trepidation was also a feeling of respect, almost of awe. They were about to step into the past, into a chamber that had been sealed for thousands of years.

When they turned the corner to take the fork to the Healer's Cove, Haan was standing there waiting for them. At his side was Artadel, the Healer.

The two Leaders nodded at each other and Haan and Artadel fell silently in behind the others, while the guards brought up the rear.

They found the area as they had left it, with Acaraho's seven guards standing watch. The High

Protector thanked them and sent them home to get some rest, ordering the new ones into place.

The Leaders each unconsciously took a deep breath as they headed toward the opening. As they passed it, they could not help but look up at the towering rock that had sealed Kthama Minor for thousands of years.

The inner boulder was itself also massive. With effort, the People would have been able to move it aside. But there was no way the People could ever have moved the first one, even if they had known there was any reason to.

One by one, they stepped inside and lined up next to each other.

Kthama Minor was appropriately named. It was on a slightly smaller scale than the Kthama they knew, but once past the entryway, it immediately seemed familiar. The ceilings were as high, and the opening chamber in which they were was nearly as large as the Great Entrance. Just as at Kthama, there were tunnels that led out of it. The group stood a while, taking in the familiar structure, overawed that they were standing where no one had stood for thousands of years.

In reverence, Adia broke the silence, "We are breathing in the last breath of the Mothoc, the Ancients. The last breath they took, thousands of years ago. There is a sense of relief filling this place —as if something that was waiting has finally been appeased."

They all took a few tentative steps forward, reverently, quietly, realizing the enormity of where they were and what they were doing.

"I suggest we go slowly and keep together. It may look like Kthama, but it is not, and we do not know if there are structural weak spots or even places where the tunnel floors might not be solid," warned Acaraho.

"We should stay in teams and not travel far in any direction," added Khon'Tor. "Let us return here soon with a report of what we have learned so far."

So the group divided, with Khon'Tor, Tehya, and Haan going in one direction and Acaraho, Adia, and Awan in the other.

As with Kthama, the tunnels were far bigger than the People needed. The whole of the interior was darker due to the large stones that partially blocked the entryway, allowing less sunlight to enter.

Acaraho and his team took the largest tunnel to the right. Several yards in, it opened to a huge area similar to Kthama's Great Chamber. He could see more hallways leading out from it, which he surmised lead to living quarters and smaller rooms. Not wanting to risk going farther, they decided to go back to the first chamber, where they had started.

Before long, Khon'Tor, Tehya, and Haan also returned.

Acaraho described what they had seen.

When he had finished, Khon'Tor said, "You all need to come this way, with us."

They followed Khon'Tor down the corridor that his party had explored. The moment Adia entered, she felt a shift again—as she had before when the Sarnonn were preparing to open Kthama Minor. She staggered, and Acaraho immediately took her arm to support her. "You should return to Kthama," he said protectively, but Adia shook her head no.

Some way on, the tunnel grew lighter, a shaft of light penetrating the darkness from somewhere in the ceiling. Beyond it was another similar opening.

"The light must be coming from a ventilation shaft," said Acaraho, squinting up to the ceiling as he tried to work out where the top opening would be. "Through all these generations, why have we never noticed it?"

Haan stepped forward. "The Fathers cloaked Kthama Minor when they sealed it."

Eyebrows rose as everyone looked at the Sarnonn Leader.

"What do you mean?" said Khon'Tor.

"Because of their role on Etera, the Mothoc had abilities that the Akassa would consider supernatural. The Sarnonn have retained some of them. One is the ability to manipulate the visual field around objects and around ourselves. In addition to the prohibition against making contact, that is why you never knew of our community, though we live relatively close to yours. The Mothoc had an additional method that also hides the energy-memory of something like Kthama Minor. When the Fathers sealed it, they also cloaked it at a level far stronger than we could have done. Otherwise, the Healers would have sensed it was here."

"I sensed *something*. This place, well the Healer's Cove, always whispered to me of mysteries and secrets. But I had no idea that there was an entire underground living system behind the Healer's Rock," said Adia quietly.

Answers that bring more questions, thought Khon'Tor. He stepped forward, beckoning the others to continue on their way. "Come. You need to see this."

He led them down the corridor to the second opening just behind the shaft of light beaming in from overhead. He stood in a vast entrance where he waited for everyone to file in.

Acaraho, Adia, and Awan stepped through and stopped dead in their tracks. Their eyes scanned the interior. Again, Adia took Acaraho's arm to keep from falling. He supported her, his concern rising to uncomfortable levels.

Returning his attention to what lay before them, Acaraho said, "We need to notify the High Council."

CHAPTER 7

Before them was the largest chamber any of them had ever seen, far larger even than Kthama's Great Chamber. The walls extended to a ceiling easily twice the height of that at Kthama. The light that came in bathed everything in a soft, warm glow. Over time, sand had drifted from the walls and now dusted the floor. No one wanted to enter, to make footprints where no one had stepped for so many generations.

Beyond comprehension in their complexity were markings that stretched from floor to ceiling and from one end of the cavern to the other. From where they were standing, they could recognize some of the symbols, and each stood transfixed, overcome with the magnitude of what they were staring at.

Khon'Tor looked at Haan.

Glancing down at Khon'Tor and then back at the giant chamber, Haan declared, "The Wall of Records.

Here lies the shame of Wrak-Wavara, the Age of Darkness."

The records of the ages. A history of the pairings between the Mothoc and the Others. It would take forever to understand it, but somewhere in here might be the answers to solve the problem of their dwindling bloodlines.

Khon'Tor looked at Acaraho, who slowly shook his head and turned to address everyone. "We must leave. I will send word to the High Council; we need Bidzel and Yuma'qia. Adia, Oh'Dar said that the Waschini have a way to record thoughts that others can understand—something he called writing?"

"Yes," she answered, still leaning against Acaraho for support.

"We need him back here by the time the High Council arrives, with or without having won back Acise. Haan, can the outer rock be replaced?"

"No, Khon'Tor. It would require us to reenter the Ror'Eckrah, and we are not up to it yet. And we might not survive opening it a third time for the High Council. But we can replace the interior rock; you could move it yourselves with an organized effort," he explained.

Khon'Tor was thinking. He hated to close it off to further exploration until the High Council arrived, but there was no way only to block off that room. "Let us leave for now. We can determine how to proceed later. Adia, you look as if you need a break. I know you said that geographic distance does not make a difference, but I do not want to take a chance on your health, or your offspring, by staying here any longer. Perhaps you and Urilla Wuti can find a way to overcome these effects."

Despite her protests, Acaraho swept Adia up and carried her out behind the others. When they were outside, Haan stepped forward, and with a deep breath, pulled the second stone into place, something that—even together—the others could not have achieved.

Once back at Kthama, Tehya immediately went to reclaim Arismae from Mapiya, and Khon'Tor escorted har back to the Leader's Quarters.

"Do you need anything? I do not want to leave you, but I feel an urgency to get word to the High Council," he said, watching Tehya put Arismae to her breast, gently cradling the offspring and patting her as she nursed.

"We will be fine, Adoeete. We have more than enough food here, and after Arismae is settled down, I will probably sleep a while," she answered.

Khon'Tor leaned in and kissed her gently. "I will be back as soon as I can.

Tehya nodded, then watched her mate walk away, wishing they were lying together alone in the dark. She was surprised at how quickly after giving birth, her ardor seemed to be returning.

Khon'Tor sought out Awan. After a brief conversation, the First Guard left to send a personal messenger to the High Council.

Oh'Dar had settled into a routine at the Brothers' village. He helped Is'Taqa and Honovi wherever possible. He joined the others in general chores, he practiced weaving, he hunted, he searched for the stones he needed for his jewelry making, and he gathered wood. He intentionally avoided Acise and Pajackok as much as possible, wanting the emotions to settle down, and hopefully, giving Acise time to realize that she still cared for him. He also frequently met with Snana to discuss what he had learned from the breeding program at Shadow Ridge. Oddly, she showed a great interest in it; unlike her sister, she was fascinated by many of the men's activities.

"How can you have learned so much so soon, Oh'Dar?" Snana asked one day as they were grooming Storm and the ponies. She was brushing Storm as high up as she could.

"I am sure it does seem as if I have learned a lot in a short while. But at Shadow Ridge, there are a great number of colts and fillies bred at any given time. So, I probably have seen more results of different combinations in a far shorter period than the Brothers would. I am anxious to see someday what Storm produces out of Windrunner's filly."

"We will all be. These are exciting times, Oh'Dar, now that you have returned," smiled the young woman.

"Each time I return from Shadow Ridge, if it is

breeding season, I will bring a stallion from a different line," he offered, as he patted Windrunner on the withers.

"Oh. Are you going back?" Snana's mood turned serious.

See, this is where I make my mistakes. When I say things like that, it sounds as if I am still confused about where I belong. All I need now is for Snana to suggest that to Acise. "I have no plans to return right now, but at some point, I am sure I will go back just for a visit. I hope that I will have a beautiful young life-walker to introduce to my Waschini family," he smiled. "And someday, offspring," he added.

Snana stopped for a moment. "What is the joining act like, Oh'Dar?" she asked quietly.

Oh'Dar's eyebrows rose. *Well, probably this is how I sounded to Ben and Grandmother that day at breakfast.*

"I do not know, Snana. I am not bonded," he said. "That is probably a topic you should bring up with your mother." *I forgot that the Brothers are more relaxed about experimentation. I know Honovi believes that Acise and Pajackok have not, but please, by the Mother, tell me she is correct.*

He quickly changed the subject. "I think we are done here for now. Thank you for your help and your company. I am going back to take care of something," he said. "Are you coming with me?"

"No, I think I will stay with Storm a while longer if you do not mind," she said. Oh'Dar nodded and trotted off.

Acise was helping her mother wash off some roots and vegetables, and looked up to see Oh'Dar in the distance. Her father had made arrangements for him to live with Isskel's family, and she knew he was making a point of staying away.

She turned her attention back to her scrubbing and was startled suddenly to find Oh'Dar standing directly in front of her.

"Oh!" she exclaimed. Honovi also stopped her work.

"May I speak with you, Acise?" Oh'Dar said, looking down at her from his considerable height.

She wiped her hands off and looked at her mother as if Honovi might know what this was about.

"What is it, Oh'Dar?" asked Acise, rather calmly.

He watched her eyes rove over him. *She seems to find me attractive, but, as my father said, there must be more than that between us.* "I would like to speak with you in the shelter," he said.

Acise's heart started pounding. For some reason, she was a little afraid. "Whatever you want to say, please say it in front of my mother, here."

"Very well. Have you joined with another?"

"*What*? You know I have not. My mother vacated the promise between Pajackok and me. You heard her."

"No. I mean, have you lain with another?"

She looked at him and frowned. "You have no right to ask that."

"I may not have a right to ask it, but I believe I have a right to know."

"What business of yours is it? Have *you*?" she snapped.

"No. I have not. And that is just the point. I *love* you. I am sorry that I made a mess of it before. But it wasn't about confusing you or rejecting you—it was about wanting to make sure I knew where I belonged and that I could do right by you. Be the life-walker you deserve."

He paused a moment, "I want to spend my life with you. I want to have a family, offspring, sit with you around our own family fire. Watch our offspring learn and grow. Watch our daughters string shells together as you did as a child. Our sons learn to ride, hunt, fish. This is not a casual infatuation for me. I have not even kissed another female since I kissed you. And I think I have the right to know whether you have kissed anyone—or more."

"And what if I have?"

Oh'Dar closed his eyes and paused. He had to turn away, to push down the hurt inside. Then he looked back at her, waiting for an answer.

"If I have, will you leave? And if I choose Pajackok again, will you leave? Go back to Shadow World?"

"Shadow Ridge," he said a little too harshly. "I cannot tell you that I will never return to Shadow

Ridge. My Waschini family is there, and I have grown to care for them. But my home is here, with the People. And with the Brothers. If and when I go back, I was hoping to take you with me, as my mate, for a visit—so that you might meet them, and they can meet you. But if you are asking me that if you choose Pajackok, will I skulk around here like a wounded puppy? Waiting for a crumb of your attention to fall my way? No, I will not. I will find someone else because I believe in being bonded. As long as there is a chance for you and me, I would never pursue another, and I want someone who feels the same about me. And that is why I deserve to know if you and Pajackok have been with each other. Because if you have, then that answers my question about your true feelings for me. I know that the People and the Brothers feel differently, but I cannot help it. I could never lie with another, with you still in my heart."

Acise looked up at Oh'Dar, tears brimming in her eyes. Oh'Dar's heart skipped a beat. *She has. She has been with Pajackok. Why else would she look at me like that?*

"I see. Well. I have my answer then, do I not?" Brokenhearted, dejected, he dropped his head, turned, and walked away.

Acise ran ahead of him and stopped, hands out. "No, wait, Oh'Dar. You misunderstand. I have not been with Pajackok. I see now that I almost made the biggest mistake of my life, nursing my wounds over your leaving me to return to Shadow Ridge. I have let the hurt I felt drive me to be dishonest about my feelings for you. I do not love Pajackok. And I have not lain with him. It is not that he did not wish it, but despite the differences in our traditions, I feel as you do. I could never lie with him while having another in my heart. It is you whom I love, Oh'Dar. And it always has been. And always will be," she cried, covering her face with her hands.

Oh'Dar leaned over and placed a hand on her bowed head. "Thank the Great Spirit," he said, and she lowered her hands and looked up at him. He leaned down, and he kissed her gently, sweetly, tasting the salt of her tears on her lips.

Honovi had her hands to her face, overcome with relief.

Oh'Dar gently wiped the tears from Acise's cheeks and stroked the hair back from her forehead. Acise let herself fall against him, and he wrapped her in his arms.

Honovi came over to them and finally managed to speak. "So, you have decided, Acise? You choose Oh'Dar?"

Acise pulled back to look up at him again. "I choose Oh'Dar of the People of the High Rocks, son of Adia, the Healer, and Acaraho, the High Protector."

"I promise I will make up for all the stupid mistakes I have made. And I will never give you another reason to doubt me—even for a moment," promised Oh'Dar.

"You can start by not fighting with Pajackok," she said.

Oh'Dar bit his tongue and did not point out that it was Pajackok who had started each brawl.

Ithua was on her way to help Honovi and Acise with the vegetables but had paused at seeing Oh'Dar approach Acise. She did not need to hear what was said to understand the outcome.

She watched the moment with bittersweet feelings. She breathed a deep sigh of relief and whispered thanks to the Great Mother. *I am glad she did not make the mistake I did. I missed out on one of the greatest blessings of life. Both my son's mate and my niece have proven wiser than I in navigating their paths.*

Suddenly Acise stiffened. "I need to tell Pajackok," she said.

"No, you do not," Pajackok announced loudly from behind, suddenly appearing. He seized Oh'Dar by the arm, jerking him away from Acise, and slammed his fist into Oh'Dar's face.

Oh'Dar stumbled but caught himself before going down. He wiped the blood from his mouth with his tunic sleeve and turned to face Pajackok.

"You seem to be making a habit of this, Pajackok. If you want to fight me, fight me fairly. Do not sneak up on me and land the first blow before I have a chance to defend myself." Acise ran to her mother, who was already looking around for Is'Taqa.

"You accuse me of being unfair? What is fair about stealing another brave's woman? Oh, but then, I forgot, you are Waschini. And the White Wasters do not shackle themselves with the inconveniences of good character."

"You cannot steal from another man something that was never his," Oh'Dar countered.

Acise was relieved that so far, it was only words, though words created harm of their own.

Before long, Honovi came racing back with Is'Taqa in tow.

"What is going on here!" he demanded, stepping between the two rivals.

"Pajackok is having a problem accepting the truth. Acise has chosen me," Oh'Dar explained, never taking his eyes off his opponent.

"Is this true, Acise? You have chosen Oh'Dar?"

"Yes, Papa. I love him. I always have. And I always will," she said, with the last declaration looking to catch Pajackok's eye to try to get through to him. "I am so sorry, Pajackok," she added.

"There is nothing to fight over. Let it go," Is'Taqa addressed Pajackok.

"I am not going to stand by and let that White Man take what was promised to me!" he snarled.

Acise could stand it no longer. She rushed over to Pajackok and yelled, "*I am not yours. I do not belong to you.*"

Pajackok pushed her aside, "Get out of my way," and started toward Oh'Dar again.

Oh'Dar saw red. "Keep your hands off her. Touch her again, and I will make you wish you had not," he shouted.

Is'Taqa sighed. He had lived long enough to know that matters such as this were best resolved sooner rather than later. It had already gone on for too long. Putting it off any longer would only let it resurface at another time—perhaps under less supervised circumstances.

Is'Taqa went to his daughter and took her arm, and led her to Honovi.

"What are you doing?" Honovi asked.

"Stay here," the Second Chief said to his daughter. "Honovi, this has gone on long enough. Like it or not, they need to fight it out. Neither appears armed, and it is better to have it done with out here in the open. They are fairly evenly matched. It is unlikely one or the other will come to any serious harm."

As before, Oh'Dar stripped off his tunic and threw it to the ground. Pajackok stripped off his, and each now down to buckskins and bare feet, they prepared to engage.

Oh'Dar kicked some stones away and emptied his mind as his father had taught him, making way for his reflexes and training to take over. As before, Pajackok's anger would give him the advantage in momentum, but it would also cloud his judgment.

In a way, Is'Taqa was wrong. It was not a fair fight. Oh'Dar had been trained not only by the Brothers but had the benefit of his father's training.

And because of Oh'Dar's smaller size, Acaraho had made sure to teach him all he could about fighting a much stronger adversary—training that would now give him the clear advantage of strategy over brute force.

Pajackok could contain his anger no longer; he charged at Oh'Dar, attempting to seize him around the waist and knock him down. Oh'Dar had seen him prepare and waited until just the right moment to step out of the way. Pajackok went sailing past and struggled to gain his balance in the mad run.

He turned, and his anger burned even hotter. "What was that, some type of Waschini trick?"

"Not at all, Pajackok. I just stepped out of the way. Just as you should now with Acise; is that a problem for you?" Oh'Dar knew the more he enraged Pajackok, the less self-control his opponent would have.

"Engage me. Fight like a man," the brave shouted, arms raised with clenched fists.

Oh'Dar shrugged and took a step toward Pajackok, who this time reached for his opponent's shoulders, hoping to wrestle him to the ground. Oh'Dar put his hands together and raised them up and outward, breaking Pajackok's hold on him. Then he brought one arm down and punched Pajackok in the midriff, knocking the air out of him.

The brave crouched on the ground, clearly feeling the blow. "What are you waiting for?"

"I am waiting for you to get up. I do not have to

use unfair advantage to win this fight. Take your time; I can wait."

For a moment, Is'Taqa was reminded of Khon'-Tor. He could also keep his cool in otherwise heated moments. He knew that Oh'Dar's calm banter was throwing his opponent off-center, and that was a great advantage.

Pajackok roared in anger and once again rushed toward Oh'Dar. This time Oh'Dar stooped down at the last moment and caught Pajackok at just the right height to roll him over and onto the ground.

"Alright. This has gone on long enough," Oh'Dar said. He dragged Pajackok to his feet, holding each of his opponent's fists at the wrist in a steely grip. "It is over now. It is time to move on. For what it is worth, I am sorry this has come between us. We used to race ponies together, go on hunting parties. I called you a friend. I would like to be able to do so again."

Pajackok squeezed his eyes shut. He jerked his hands to free them and stormed over to retrieve his tunic, dusting it off before putting it on. He threw Oh'Dar a sour look.

"You should never have come back," he shouted. He took a last look at Acise, turned and stomped off.

Honovi breathed a sigh of relief as Acise ran into Oh'Dar's arms. "That could have been a lot worse."

"I am not sure it is over yet. We should keep our wits about us for a while," said Is'Taqa as he and Honovi walked over to the couple.

"Let us not dwell on what has just happened. When would you like the ceremony, Acise?"

Acise looked up into Oh'Dar's eyes. "As soon as possible, please."

Oh'Dar said, "I need to go and tell my parents. Acise, would you go with me?"

"Of course!"

"Thank you. My father told me not to come home until I had won your heart." That made everyone laugh.

Behind them, they heard a commotion as several maidens excitedly approached Ithua. The Healer listened a moment, then turned toward Is'Taqa and the others.

"Come quickly," she called. "Chief Ogima has collapsed!"

The Chief had just been discovered in his shelter in a heap on the ground by two of the village maidens when they brought him something to eat. They had rolled him onto his sleeping blanket before running for help.

Ithua was the first one in and crouched by his side. She lifted his eyelids, felt his temperature, his pulse. She put an ear to his chest to gauge his breathing and gently opened his mouth to check the color of his gums.

He was unresponsive to all.

"He appears to have suffered some type of episode. Whether he will come out of it, I do not know. All we can do now is keep him warm, speak gently to him, and wait. And pray," added Ithua.

Oh'Dar asked, "Do you want me to bring my mother? She cannot do more than you can, but she might be a comfort to you. And Khon'Tor and my father will want to know."

Ithua thought for a moment, then looked at Is'Taqa, Second Chief. "If they can come, I believe they would want to; in my heart, I have little hope that he will recover."

"I do not know if Khon'Tor's mate will come," said Oh'Dar. "She does not know him, and she may wish to stay home with Arismae, their daughter."

"Daughter? Khon'Tor has a daughter?"

"Did I not tell you?"

"Oh'Dar!" exclaimed Honovi.

"Oh, I apologize. I have been so upset about Acise. A great deal has happened, and after things settle down, I will tell you all about it."

Honovi shook her head at him, but she understood.

Oh'Dar turned to Acise, "Would you prefer to ride behind me or alongside on one of the ponies?"

"I can ride behind. If you do not mind having my arms wrapped around you," she said with a smile.

With Chief Ogima Adoeete lying there facing an uncertain future, Oh'Dar felt ashamed at the pictures that ran through his mind.

Before long, Acise and Oh'Dar were ready to head for Kthama. He knew the watchers would send word ahead, and his parents would be waiting for them by the time they arrived.

Oh'Dar mounted Storm, then helped Acise up, placing her in front of him instead of behind.

"I feel it is safer if you are in front of me. You can hold onto Storm's mane, and I will keep one arm around you." He snuggled her up against him, slipped his arm around her waist, and then they were off.

Though Oh'Dar knew time was of the essence, with two of them, there was only so fast he was willing to let Storm go. But he was right; when they arrived, not only his father and mother were there waiting for him, but also Nadiwani, Nootau, Nimida, and Mapiya. Khon'Tor and Tehya were present as well.

He brought Storm up to a stop and turned him. Acaraho reached up to help lift Acise down. Within moments she was surrounded by well-wishers, all big smiles and congratulations.

When it died down a bit, Khon'Tor approached Oh'Dar. "I am glad to see you back home. And I can see your—mission—was successful. Your father explained it to me."

Adia gently embraced Acise. "Welcome to the family. We could not be happier."

"Nor I," Acise replied.

"Oh'Dar, when is the pairing ceremony to be?" his mother asked.

"We wanted it as soon as possible, but now—I am sorry, but something tragic has happened." The mood instantly changed from joviality to one of rapt attention.

"Chief Ogima Adoeete has collapsed. Ithua does not have much hope for his recovery. We came to tell you of our upcoming pairing, but also to deliver this sad but urgent news."

Khon'Tor was silent. He and the Chief had been allies for a long time. After Khon'Tor's father died, it was Chief Ogima who had counseled him in many times of need. At one stage, the Chief was the closest thing to a friend that Khon'Tor had.

"I will go to see him."

"I will stay here, Khon'Tor. We will watch over Tehya for you." Acaraho knew Adia was not well enough to travel, and he could see by the saddened look on her face that she knew it too.

"Yes, I cannot make the journey at this time. I am so sorry. I am sure Ithua could use my support, and I hate to let her down," said Adia.

"Are you alright, Mama?" Oh'Dar was immediately concerned.

"A lot has happened, Oh'Dar. For one, I am seeded."

Oh'Dar ran over and hugged her, then hugged Acaraho. He slapped Nootau on the back, "We are going to be big brothers." He turned to Adia. "We must be on our way then. Mama, is there anything you wish to send with us?"

"Only my love to Ithua—and my deepest regrets. Please tell her I am carrying an offspring and do not feel well; she will understand why I cannot come."

Khon'Tor turned to Oh'Dar. "I will meet you there."

Oh'Dar mounted and helped Acise up, and then they were off.

Khon'Tor walked back to his mate and discreetly hugged her. He tilted her chin up with his finger so he could look into her eyes. "I do not wish to leave you. But in this case, I must."

"I understand. This is important. I will be fine."

Adia walked over and put her arm around Tehya. "Would you like one of us to stay with you until he returns? Or you are welcome to stay in the Healer's Quarters, and we can all sleep there together?"

Tehya thought for a moment. Her nightmares had not stopped, and without Khon'Tor next to her, she did not know how she would do. She only felt safe when he was with her.

"I think I would like to have you stay with me, Adia. And Acaraho, if that is alright."

"That is not a problem. We will move our sleeping mats in shortly."

"Wait! I have an idea," said Nimida. "We should all sleep in the Workshop. It would be a sleeping party."

Nadiwani saw Tehya's reluctance. "That is a great

idea, Nimida. The rest of us could. But for now, I think Tehya would be more comfortable in her quarters, with Arismae and Adia."

"Oh. I did not think of that. Of course. But maybe another time?"

Adia was glad to see her unclaimed daughter so happy. *She has come a long way since joining us. She smiles now; she relaxes and jokes.*

Khon'Tor made it to the village ahead of Oh'Dar and Acise. He stood in the treeline for a while before moving forward. He knew that his sudden appearance would frighten them, and he wished he could warn them of his approach.

Is'Taqa, Noshoba, and Snana were sitting around the family fire when Khon'Tor stepped out of the shadows. Snana could not help herself. His sudden appearance startled her, and she screamed and ran to her father's arms.

Is'Taqa immediately recognized Khon'Tor, even in the dark, by the white streak and his imposing build. He calmed his daughter, then told her to find her mother. Snana hurried off, her feet slapping the ground, occasionally turning to look back at the imposing figure standing next to her father and little brother.

Noshoba would have gone with Snana except that he could not move. He was awestruck.

"Am I too late?" Khon'Tor asked Is'Taqa.

"He is still with us, though in and out of consciousness. Ithua said his heartbeat is erratic. She believes he will not be here much longer. Come with me, please."

Is'Taqa started to lead Khon'Tor but noticed his son still sitting by the fire. "Do you wish to come, son?"

Noshoba managed to shake his head no, his mouth still hanging open.

"This way."

Khon'Tor had to stoop considerably to enter Chief Ogima's shelter. He moved slowly toward the Chief and crouched down, still an imposing figure.

He placed his hand very gently on the Chief's chest and bowed his head. "Hello, old friend," he said.

Chief Ogima stirred a bit at hearing Khon'Tor's voice and weakly opened his eyes. He moved his hand slowly, resting it over Khon'Tor's. In the background, the slow rhythm of the deathwatch drums continued, ritually creating a passage to the Great Spirit's world through which the Chief could pass.

"Yes to old, and yes to friend. I fear I have not much time left here, Khon'Tor. I am glad you have come to bid me a good journey."

Despite himself, tears stung the back of Khon'-Tor's eyes.

"I am proud of you. You are indeed the great Leader I knew you to be. And I know you will be the friend to Is'Taqa that you have been to me. I have walked the long path set before me. And I am tired. In many ways, I am glad to be at the end of it."

"The People will always be friends to the Brothers. Tehya and I have a daughter, Adoeete. We have named her Arismae. And Adia is seeded. She and Acaraho are very excited. There is finally lasting and solid peace among the leadership of the People. And now our tribes will be further joined, as Oh'Dar and Acise are to be paired."

The Chief nodded slowly, patting Khon'Tor's hand. "I am sorry that our path together must end, but glad that you bring me such happy news to carry me on my way. Continue without me in peace, my friend."

Chief Ogima patted Khon'Tor's hand again, then closed his eyes and turned his head. He let out a long sigh, and his body seemed to sink farther into the colorful sleeping blanket under him.

Khon'Tor stood crouched there for a while; the Chief had fallen asleep. He carefully removed his hand and pulled the blanket up,—a gesture of care not lost on the witnesses in the room. "Good journey, my friend. Until our paths meet up again in the House of the Great Spirit."

Khon'Tor discreetly pinched the bridge of his nose, stopping the sting of tears, before turning and standing up.

"It will not be long now," said Ithua. "I think he was waiting for you, Khon'Tor. Those are the first words he has spoken since he collapsed."

"I will miss him. More than I can find the words

to say. He was a great leader. An inspiration to me, a teacher. In many ways, a father."

Khon'Tor turned to Is'Taqa. He reached out and rested his hand on Is'Taqa's shoulder. Is'Taqa knew this was a great honor. He returned the gesture as best he could, resting his hand on Khon'Tor's bicep.

"As Second Chief, the mantle will pass to you now, Is'Taqa. My people and I will help you, however we can. I hope in time, despite my great failings, that you will also come to call me friend."

Oh'Dar and Acise had caught up by then and were standing in the doorway watching Khon'Tor bid farewell to his counterpart and pass their vow of friendship to Is'Taqa.

In the corner in the back, Ithua sat huddled, glad for the privacy provided by the cover of darkness. Finally, one by one, they left, leaving her alone with the great Chief. She moved to his side and placed her hands over his.

She looked at him lying so quiet and still, and she caressed his face. She spoke to him softly, "My greatest mistake was that I chose the path other than the one you offered me, the one that led to your heart. I am sorry that I passed up the chance to stand by your side as your life-walker. I never stopped loving you. And I never will. Perhaps we will be together on the other side. Forgive me, my beloved, for my foolishness and pride that denied us both a lifetime of love."

The Chief stirred a moment, and then every part of him relaxed. The room became deathly still.

He was gone.

Ithua leaned forward and pressed her lips to his for the second and last time. She brought the edges of the blanket up around him, the blanket she had made for him so long ago. Then she reverently extinguished the flame of the watch light. As the light faded, outside the drums slowed, then ceased.

"So sorry. I am so sorry." She dropped her head to rest on his still chest.

From outside the shelter several yards away, the small group was still assembled and talking quietly amongst themselves. They heard Ithua's heartbreaking wails coming from within the Chief's shelter.

Honovi and Is'Taqa looked at each other, and Is'Taqa frowned. He knew that his sister cared about the Chief. She always made a point of looking after him—but she cared for everyone.

"Your sister loved him. And he loved her. Did you not know?" Honovi asked softly.

Is'Taqa shook his head slowly.

"That she did not bond with him will always be her greatest regret. I do not know that he ever stopped asking her. Even recently. But she always refused. Someday, perhaps I will ask her why. Did you not ever wonder why he was ministered to by the village women and had no life-walker of his own? He was still waiting for her. Even now, until his last breath. He was waiting for her."

Acise turned her head and stared out into the dark forest surrounding them, now understanding Ithua's warning to her several weeks back, "*Regret is a hard master, Acise.*"

Khon'Tor quietly listened to the women.

"Will you be staying?" Honovi asked him.

"No. I will make my way back. I have frightened enough of your children for one visit, I believe."

He glanced back at Is'Taqa's fire. Noshoba was still sitting there. He turned a little more and could see Snana in the doorway of the shelter.

"Oh'Dar?" asked Khon'Tor.

"I know you wish me to return. I will within a day or so, I promise. I am needed here at the moment."

"As you will, then." Khon'Tor nodded to the rest and left, being careful to give both Noshoba and the shelter a wide berth.

Back at Kthama, the mats had been arranged in the Leader's Quarters so that Acaraho and Adia could spend the night with Tehya. Once Arismae was settled in her nest, Adia moved to the sleeping mat that had been placed next to Tehya's. Kweeuu slipped onto Tehya's mat and lay next to her, as was his custom.

"We are right here, Tehya," whispered Adia. "Acaraho is between us and the door. There are two guards outside, two of Acaraho's best males. No one can get to you. You are safe." She scooted over and opened her arms. Tehya hugged her, and the Healer held the Leader's mate as a mother would hold a young offspring. She patted Tehya's back, even rocked her a bit.

"It is alright. You are safe. No one will let anyone harm you ever again. Rest. You need to rest," Adia softly said as she continued to stroke Tehya's hair and soothe her.

Acaraho knew his mate was exhausted too. But true to her calling, she would not put her needs above another's.

Before too long, Tehya was sleeping soundly, and Adia also let herself drift off.

Not much later, the Healer opened her eyes. She had dreamed of Chief Ogima. He was standing before her in a beautiful forest, his Chief's staff in his hand. He was strong, robust. A much younger version of himself—a version she had never known. He smiled at her, nodded, then turned and walked away, disappearing into the fog. She knew at that moment that Chief Ogima Adoeete had returned to the Great Spirit.

Is'Taqa is now Chief of the Brothers.

Khon'Tor took his time returning to Kthama, taking in the sanctity of the night. The moon had disappeared beneath the horizon, and the stars burned brightly overhead.

As he walked, he thought back to the years he had shared with the Chief. Khon'Tor remembered when Ogima's father had died, and he became the Brothers' Chief. He remembered Ogima's mother also passing, years later. Chief Ogima Adoeete had never paired, which Khon'Tor finally understood. The Chief must have had his choice of any of the females. Yet he had never paired because he was holding out for the one he loved but who, for some reason, would not join with him.

I never knew that. It is almost too sad to bear. Everything reminds me of how precious love is, how blessed I am to have Tehya.

There had been many meetings, High Council meetings, meetings that had affected both their tribes. Chief Ogima had stood with Khon'Tor at the farewell ritual of Khon'Tor's father. Together, they had learned of the Wrak-Ayya. Chief Ogima Adoeete had been at Kthama when Hakani kidnapped Oh'Dar and dangled him dangerously over her head while trying to cause trouble for Adia. The Chief had been the one to admonish him for not admitting his crimes against Adia, but true to his nature, he had done so by appealing to Khon'Tor's potential for greatness. Reminded him of who he used to be—or could be.

Another season of my life has closed. So many recently. Hakani is gone—this time for good. Acaraho and Adia are finally together, as they should be. Tehya—my Tehya, I almost lost her. And now there is Arismae. What lies ahead, I have no way of knowing. We still have to face the Wrak-Ayya. And there is the matter of Haan's people. And the secrets of Kthama Minor. And Akar. I must find out what happened to Akar. If he still lives, I must finish what I should have done long ago. I have to pray that I can somehow reach Haan—make him understand that I must do what I must do—before I track down his son.

Khon'Tor made it back to Kthama in the middle of the night. But, considering the time, he did not want to disturb or frighten anyone in his quarters.

Once again, he found the spot he had chosen so many years earlier. The night air was chilly, so he gathered fir branches for padding and cover. Finally settled, he stretched out. As he looked up at the night sky before closing his eyes to sleep, a shooting star streaked brightly across the dark background.

Khon'Tor smiled. *Goodbye, old friend. Safe passage home.*

CHAPTER 8

The next morning, Tehya for once awoke refreshed. She had slid down on the mat, as had Adia, and the Healer was cuddled up around her. Tehya looked across the room to see the High Protector lying on his mat, watching her and Adia.

Acaraho had been awake for a while but remained on his mat in front of the entrance to avoid waking the females. As Tehya looked around, he thought she looked rested and hoped they had both had a good night's sleep.

I wonder how Urilla Wuti is doing, and when Oh'Dar will return. It did not sound hopeful for Chief Ogima Adoeete. It feels like he is gone. I wish I could have said goodbye, but it was important that Khon'Tor went. And neither he nor I would have felt comfortable with both of us leaving.

Acaraho's thoughts turned to the High Council

members. *Word has gone out, and they should be here within a few days. Because they are our best chance at deciphering the markings on the Wall of Records, Khon'Tor specifically requested Bidzel and Yuma'qia also come.*

Adia stirred and stretched, unwrapping herself from Tehya. She smoothed back Tehya's hair, "Are you awake?"

"Yes. And so is your mate. He has been staring at us from across the room for some time now," Tehya smiled. "That was the best sleep I have had in a long while."

"Are you hungry?" asked Adia. "Shall we go to the Great Chamber, or would you like me to scavenge around in here?"

"If you do not mind, scavenge away."

"Sure, here I go." And the Healer patted Tehya on the arm as she arose.

Adia stepped around the sleeping mats and walked over to Arismae's nest. She was sleeping soundly. Then she walked over to Acaraho, who was now feigning sleep. As she approached him, he slipped his arm out and grabbed her ankle then one hand, and dragged her down on top of him.

"Acaraho!" she laughed.

"Good Morning," he said, rolling her over and under him, then kissing her passionately. Her face was red, but her pulse was racing. Then he released her to go on her way. As she stood up, he slapped her on her behind.

She scowled at him, to which he just laughed.

"Do not look at me like that, female," he said. "I am just happy this morning. I know that sounds insensitive. But the Chief's illness has reminded me of what is important in this life. His journey has ended. My heart is sad and yet full of gratitude that we have ours ahead of us for many, many years. And soon, our family will be expanded."

Adia did not tell Acaraho about her dream, but she would later. She padded the rest of the way to the eating area and started poking around.

Within a few moments, the stone door moved. Immediately, Acaraho was on his feet. "Good Morning?"

It was Khon'Tor.

Kweeuu wagged his tail, and Tehya sat up, waiting for her mate to come through the door. She reached her arms out to him, beckoning him to come and sit with her.

"Oh'Dar will not return for a few days," said the Leader as he sat down next to Tehya. "Did you sleep?"

"Like a well-fed offspring," Tehya answered.

"I am relieved to hear that. How do you feel?"

"I did not have any nightmares last night, Adoeete. Perhaps the spell is broken, and they will not come back."

"We were not sure when you would return," said Acaraho.

"The Chief crossed over last night. I am glad I

went, but there was no need for me to remain. I was only going to cause disruption during a time of reverence."

Acaraho nodded. Adia paused in her rummaging around the food area.

"Is'Taqa is now First Chief," said Khon'Tor.

"Is that good?" asked Tehya, though she was sure she knew the answer.

"It is good. He is a worthy soul, and he will make a fine leader. Cooperation between our people is still assured for many years to come."

Adia had found an interesting combination of foodstuffs and brought some to each of them.

"Thank you. When do you expect the High Council members to arrive?" Khon'Tor asked Acaraho.

"Within a few days. I will need to focus on getting living quarters ready for them. And we should let Haan know." Acaraho stopped chewing. "I had completely forgotten about Haaka. Does anyone know how she is?"

"She was with us when we entered Kthama Minor. I did not sense any alarm or concern from her. I believe she is enjoying her stay here. Something tells me she does not want to leave," said Adia, finally sitting down with her meal.

Acaraho tossed something to Kweeuu, who caught it mid-flight.

Adia spoke again. "I am going to check on Haaka, then refresh myself in the females' bathing area. The waters should not be quite as cold now, with Etera waking."

Before he left with his mate, Acaraho suggested to Khon'Tor that he update the community. "No doubt they are feeling some level of alarm. The last time you addressed them, we asked everyone to stay in their quarters and pray."

Khon'Tor nodded. "Yes, I need to let them know that Kthama Minor has been opened and that Chief Ogima has returned to the Great Spirit."

With that, the others left Khon'Tor and Tehya to their day.

Adia could not locate Haaka in the eating area, so went to the Sarnonn's quarters. Haaka invited her in and seemed glad to see her.

"I wanted to check on you. Are you alright so far? Is Kalli well?"

"We are fine. I miss Haan, but otherwise, I am content here. I wanted to ask if there is anything I can do to make up for my keep?"

"That is kind of you to offer, Haaka, but it is not necessary. Just relax and enjoy your stay. I know that where you and Haan's following will go after this must weigh on you."

"They are fine in the meadow above for now, but yes, we will need a home of our own."

Adia put her hand on the female's arm. "I understand. I am going to relax in the females' bathing area. It is deep enough that if you wish, you could soak your whole body. I do not suppose that is something you would enjoy?"

Haaka frowned at the thought of the long period necessary for her sopping wet body-covering to dry. "It sounds pleasurable, perhaps, for an Akassa," she replied.

Adia smiled.

"Do you ever have fires at Kthama?" Haaka asked.

"If you mean outside as the Brothers do, no, not as a matter of course. With permission, we sometimes have small ones inside to heat medicine. Khon'Tor does not allow them otherwise. Improperly done, they can fill the hallways with smoke, and it is difficult to clear. Why?"

"I thought I saw one the other night, coming back after Kthama Minor was opened."

Adia blinked. *It could not have been one of our people. And Haan's were all present, having been occupied in whatever collective trance they were in.* The thought that entered her mind made her blood run cold.

"I will mention it to Khon'Tor. He may wish to ask you more about it," said Adia finally.

Haaka hesitated. "Adia, before you go, is there any chance we might be allowed to stay at Kthama?"

Adia could feel the longing coming off of Haaka along with the question and was immediately saddened.

"I do not know, Haaka. But whatever happens

next, we will help you and your people find a home. We were separated by our past, and now we are joined by our future. Are you missing Kayerm?"

"No, not really. It is much different here; everything is so—organized. You work together. Meals are prepared, the males hunt together to provide for everyone, not just their pods. It is a true community. Now that I see how it is at Kthama, I realize living at Kayerm was surviving, but it was not enjoyable."

The longer she stays, the harder it will be for her to leave.

Khon"Tor called an assembly that afternoon. It took longer for the Great Chamber to fill as they had remained sequestered as he had asked them. Once everyone was seated, he took the floor.

He raised his left hand to speak, as was his custom.

"No doubt you have spent the last few days in some state of alarm. But despite your fears, I thank you for your prayers. We have passed the worst of it. Kthama Minor is open. Now we await the High Council's arrival to explore it further. I will give you a fuller report once we have more of an idea of what awaits us there. For now, I will only say that it is much like our home here. Its existence is a shock to all of us."

He paused, "On a sadder note, Chief Ogima

Adoeete of the Brothers has returned to the Great Spirit. Chief Ogima led the Brothers with integrity, wisdom, and love, and he left a legacy of peace between our people. I called him friend. I have no doubt his successor, Chief Is'Taqa, will lead with the same fine character. Our good relations will continue under his leadership.

"Please continue to pray periodically for Kthama, as the Healers explained when we last assembled, but otherwise, you may return to your normal activities."

Then Khon'Tor stepped closer and asked, "Does anyone have any specific concerns that need to be addressed?"

Pakuna stood up. "Please, Khon'Tor, what happened when Kthama Minor was opened? What was the heavy vibration we all felt, and the rocks and debris that fell from the ceiling? Is Kthama safe?"

The Leader spoke, "You all remember Haan, the Leader of the Sarnonn. And you know that one of their females, Haaka, is among us with Kalli, Haan's daughter by Hakani. Haan and his followers have been preparing to open Kthama Minor for some time. They worked in unison to open the cave, and it was their moving in a ritual formation that caused Etera to shudder. It has passed. There is nothing to be worried about. We are on good terms with Haan and his people, and we look forward to a mutually beneficial relationship.

"But this is a momentous period for us,"

Khon'Tor continued. "Learning of the Sarnonn was unnerving, I will admit. And then to find there was another part of Kthama—one of which we had no knowledge—was equally unsettling. We are learning that our understanding of some of our history has been inaccurate. After the High Council arrives and we have time to explore it further, I will give you more information. As to standing in the entrance, it was eerie. Knowing we were entering places in which no one had set foot for thousands of years left us all with a great feeling of reverence. It is with that same reverence that we will explore it in more detail."

He stood for a moment, then raised his left hand.

"The High Council should be here within a few days. You will notice preparations for their arrival. Again, if you see Haaka, please make her feel welcome. I know the Sarnonn's presence can be unnerving. But remember that she is the outsider here, and could use some kindness and hospitality.

"Thank you. That is all." Khon'Tor dropped his hand and stepped down. He had hardly left the raised platform when he was met by Adia.

"Khon'Tor, I checked on Haaka. She said she saw a fire the night we opened Kthama Minor. I thought you should know."

"I know already; the First Guard told me."

"Did they see who had lit it?"

"By the time they arrived, it had been put out, and whoever set it had left. It was a regular pit fire, self-contained, and properly extinguished. It offered no threat."

Whether it was because of her condition or because of the opening of Kthama Minor, Adia's seventh sense had become far more sensitive. She could feel several lines of worry radiating off of Khon'Tor. She also knew that he had the same idea as she about who had lit the fire.

Khon'Tor changed the subject. "Why do you think Tehya slept well last night?"

"It might have just been exhaustion," she said.

Khon'Tor had his own theory, but he kept it to himself.

"I am off to find Urilla Wuti, then," said Adia. "So much has been happening. I can feel she is alright, but I need to visit her."

Urilla Wuti was still in the Healer's Quarters. Adia approached quietly in case she was sleeping, but the older Healer opened her eyes and reached up to take Adia's hand.

"Join me. Please."

Adia sat down, Urilla Wuti's hand in hers. "Have you been able to rest? To clear yourself?"

"I have. You entered Kthama Minor."

"A few of us, yes. Acaraho, Khon'Tor, Tehya, Haan, and Awan were also there. We found a huge chamber at the back, with markings covering all the walls. It was both awe-inspiring and frightening. We are waiting for the High Council to arrive before we return."

"There is more. There is something more. Waiting. I cannot yet quite seem to be myself again."

"I am also having trouble. And I am picking up feelings from people left and right. I am not sure I want it to continue."

"Let us practice together again. Perhaps our combined efforts will prove more successful."

The Brothers were gathered around the body of their revered leader, Chief Ogima Adoeete. He had been laid in their sacred burial place, and ceremonial fires rimmed the exterior. The entire village was in mourning. Is'Taqa was feeling the weight of the Chief's mantle. He had served alongside the High Chief; now, he bore the responsibility alone. His mate, Honovi, stood next to him and the rest of their family slightly behind.

"Today, we bid safe journey to our beloved Chief. He was an inspiration to me and us all. He is with the Great Spirit now, but our memories of his guidance and his words of wisdom remain. As the days and years pass, in times of need, be still. Watch. Listen. He will continue to guide and help us, as he always has."

Many of the tribe did not linger; their grief was

too heavy. The fires continued to burn, the flames licking up high into the sky, the glow illuminating the tear-streaked faces of those who remained.

Ithua stood at the back. She had not been able to get her grief under control. What she had hidden all these years was finally coming to light. Her love for him was no longer a secret, as though the shell around her heart that had held while he was alive and had concealed her longing for him had been cracked open upon his death. *Too late. Too late. My only hope now is that my mistake will serve others. And that we will be together in the next life.*

Ithua's thoughts returned to the first time they had spoken of their feelings for each other. They were young. He was a new Chief; she was just starting to answer her calling as Medicine Woman. Time seemed to stretch out before them like a beautiful winding path with no end. They did not need to decide right now, she had said. There was time. And then one day turned to another, and another. Then years passed. Now decades. What had held her back? She did not know. As wise as she was supposed to be, she now realized that she had passed up what mattered most—a chance to share life's joys and heartaches with one other person. To raise a family.

Was it ambition that had kept her from his side? Duty, perhaps. A sense of unworthiness, maybe. She had believed that, in time, he would choose another. But he never had. And so her choices had brought her here—alone with the blossom of her youth passed. No family with whom to sit around an evening fire. No memories of sweet love-making under cover of the soft glades. No children to pass down the stories of their father's valor and wisdom. She had instead chosen a life of solitude; now one she would live in regret until her own time on Etera came to a close

Why did I keep refusing him? Too late, I have learned that there is not always one more chance waiting around the next turn.

Ithua thought of Adia. *I am glad my friend did not make my mistake. Despite what Khon'Tor did to her, she has still found happiness. I envy her and Acaraho for their lifetime of love and companionship. And I am relieved that Acise has chosen Oh'Dar.*

Eventually, the last to remain solemnly wandered away. Finally spotting Ithua, Is'Taqa approached and handed her the Chief's sleeping blanket. The one she had made for him so many years ago.

Tears fell as she clutched it to her.

"I am sorry, sister. I did not know. But I am told he loved you too." Ithua nodded and slowly walked away beyond the fires and into the dark. She found a spot on a mossy knoll and lay down. There she stayed until only the faintest of embers still glowed, and only her quiet sobbing broke the stillness of the night.

Unbeknownst to her, her brother, the new Chief, stayed watch in the shadows, making sure no harm came to her as she let the shell that had encased her heart break open the rest of the way.

The next morning, Oh'Dar and Acise discussed returning to Kthama with her parents.

"I want to stay, and yet I feel a need to return, but I do not wish to leave you or take Acise away at this moment."

"Trust your instincts. If you are feeling pressure to return, there is most likely a reason for that," said Honovi.

"I am. I am feeling a great urgency to get back to Kthama. Acise, would you prefer to stay here, or go with me? I do not want to take you away from your parents if you would rather stay. There is so much going on all at once," he said.

"I would rather stay here, Oh'Dar. But come back to me as soon as you can. We will wait for all this to settle before we are bonded," she replied.

Oh'Dar did not want to leave just now, with Pajackok perhaps still angry. "Is'Taqa—about Pajackok—"

"I will watch for him. Acise, please stay clear of him."

"I have no desire to interact with Pajackok," said Acise. "The sooner he forgets about me, the better."

Oh'Dar went to retrieve Storm, but before mounting the black stallion, he pressed his lips against Acise's. "When I return, I will tell you all the news that we did not have time for, and anything I can about the High Council visit."

He spurred Storm on and was gone.

Dorn and Tarnor stood before those who were left at Kayerm.

"Haan and his followers have left," said Tarnor. "Kayerm is ours now. The Rah-hora has been broken, but we will have no dealings with the Akassa. Hopefully, the repercussions will follow Haan and his usurpers, as it was his doing."

Nobody noticed that off in the distance, a lone figure, backlit by the rising sun, watched from a high spot overlooking Kayerm's entrance. No one noticed him standing up, nor did they notice as he slowly slipped away and disappeared over the ridge.

Acaraho had made the necessary arrangements for their stay by the time messengers brought word that the High Council members were close. Word had been sent through the community through the informal channels, and tensions were still high. Acaraho noted that many were spending more time in their quarters instead of outside or congregating in Kthama's communal areas.

Khon'Tor reached as far as he could. He found purchase on a small ledge and hauled himself up. He stood up and looked around. It was the highest he had ever climbed. His eyes swept the horizon where the People's land reached to the sky. *We have lived here for thousands of years. May we live here for thousands more. Grant me the wisdom to guide my people through whatever is next to come.*

After a moment's rest, he began his descent. Tired and sweaty by the time he reached the bottom, he cleansed himself in the river shallows and stretched out to dry. He lay on the soft grass, his arm sheltering his eyes from the early morning sun. Songbirds filled the air. A doe watched him from the tree line, her ears flicking back and forth. The rays on his skin were warm, comforting. He enjoyed the fatigue in his muscles, knowing that each climb was building his strength.

He thought about Haan and his followers, relieved that they had not so far had any contact from those who had not supported him. From what Haan said, Kthama Minor is isolated from Kthama. *Could they move in there—after we have explored it and learned what we need? Our people would still need access, especially to the Wall of Records, but if we are to work together, it would be convenient to have them so close. Though, alliances can fall.*

Khon'Tor sighed.

The truth is, as Acaraho said. If they wanted to take Kthama from us, they could have done so. They still could, but they approached us as allies, not as conquerors. There is no telling about the other faction. Adia said that Haaka does not want to leave—that life at Kthama is far easier than at Kayerm. If word of that should get back to the other Sarnonn, they might not respect our claim here. In which case, Haan and his group would help even out the balance of strength.

He had decided and rose to continue his return to Kthama.

I will speak to the others in my Circle of Counsel; then, if we agree, I will present it to the High Council. Ultimately, Kthama Minor is ours, and it is my decision, but in the interest of unity, I would prefer to have their agreement.

Khon'Tor turned as he was about to step into the Great Entrance; a rider was approaching.

As he stood waiting for Oh'Dar to reach him, Khon'Tor was thinking that for a Waschini, Oh'Dar had turned into a striking young male. The Leader raised his hand in greeting as the young man turned Storm to stop in front of him. "I do not see Acise this time."

"She wanted to stay with her parents. It is a time of great sadness."

Khon'Tor nodded. "Get settled quickly; I am calling a meeting and need you in attendance."

Before long, Khon'Tor and his Circle of Counsel were again assembled in the meeting room. This time, everyone was there—Acaraho, Adia, Nadiwani, Awan, Mapiya, and Oh'Dar. Tehya sat next to her mate with Arismae cradled in her arms. Adia sat with Urilla Wuti, her arm supporting the older Healer, who was not recovering from the effects quite as quickly as her younger counterpart.

"The High Council will be here shortly," Khon'Tor began. "Before they arrive, I want your thoughts. After we have had time to explore Kthama Minor and barring some unforeseen change of events, I intend to turn it over to Haan and his band."

It did not come as a surprise to any of them. At some point, they had all discussed it, either with Khon'Tor or among themselves. They did not need Kthama Minor, and it would go a long way toward helping Haan and cementing their alliance.

"I have no problem with it," said Acaraho. "It is an obvious solution. They are displaced, and our futures are being woven together. They could take it if they wanted, yet they have not even asked. That speaks well of their intentions toward us. We do not need the space, but we do need their good will."

The First Guard concurred, "Once we have learned what we need, yes, it would be better in the long run."

"It would certainly not work for them to share Kthama," said Adia. "Because they are so much larger than we are, there could always be an element of intimidation among our people, like it or not, because some reactions are visceral and cannot be overcome by reason. This seems the perfect solution, truly."

The others nodded their agreement.

"I will present my decision to the High Council," Khon'Tor said. "Based on the overwhelming response at the last community meeting, I do not expect disagreement about helping the Sarnonn, but I would prefer to have the People's support. We have much to do together to solve our problems, let alone helping the Sarnonn with theirs. Does anyone have anything else to share?" he asked.

"Haaka will be relieved," Adia answered. "It will not be quite the same, but if they are willing to learn, we can help them organize themselves. Having the Mother Stream is a great benefit, but it is the organization and sense of community she does not want to give up."

"Let us make sure we explore Kthama Minor as much as we can. I want to make sure that there are no connecting tunnels between the two. It is doubtful, I cannot imagine that there is any part of Kthama of which we are unaware," said Awan.

"I do not believe there is either," said Khon'Tor, "unless it is cloaked, as Haan says is somehow possible. But I will ask Haan directly. I do not believe he has ever lied to me and do not believe he would about this either. He has consistently expressed concern for our safety."

"Oh'Dar," Khon'Tor continued, "We discovered a chamber with markings on the wall. Haan called it the Wall of Records. I am hoping you might be able to help us understand it. You once said the Waschini have a detailed system of recording information, and your experience might prove helpful. I have asked that Bidzel and Yuma'qia return here with the High Council. They are responsible for recommending the pairings, and I have high hopes that they will understand the markings."

He looked around at each person there. "If there is nothing else, let us adjourn and prepare to visit Kthama Minor before the High Council arrives."

The group assembled—Khon'Tor, Acaraho, Awan, Adia, and Oh'Dar. Nadiwani and Tehya had stayed behind, as did Urilla Wuti. Though Urilla Wuti hated to miss out on anything so historic, she simply could not shake the dis-ease she was feeling. Khon'Tor had sent a messenger asking for Haan to join them.

As they approached Kthama Minor, Adia again felt a shift but said nothing. They entered with reverence, still mindful that until a few days before, no one had stepped foot inside for thousands of years.

There had been enough time to assimilate their first experience, and now they were each more collected—more aware and better able to observe their surroundings.

Dust and other accumulation from over the ages crunched underfoot. Each step carried them deeper into history. This time when they split up, each team went farther into the first tunnels with instructions to stay together in their small groups.

Haan led the way for Khon'Tor and Awan. As the tunnels snaked deeper into the mountainside, they could hardly tell that they were not in Kthama.

Khon'Tor could feel humidity rising from the lower levels. "The Mother Stream must also run through here?" he said, surprised.

"Yes," said Haan. "It is a great resource, as we have seen with Kthama."

Khon'Tor turned to Awan. "We must not go much farther without a way of marking our return. Let us backtrack to the main chambers to meet up with the others."

Acaraho and Adia appeared shortly, both a bit agitated. Adia was wavering on her feet, and she stepped away from the group to lean against one of the smooth walls, her hand to her head.

"This is affecting Adia greatly, Khon'Tor," the High Protector said, looking over his shoulder at his mate. "I do not like it."

"I understand. And even more so as she is carrying your offspring," said Khon'Tor. "Perhaps you should take her back to Kthama and Nadiwani."

Adia could see they were discussing her and guessed at the conversation. "I am fine. Please, continue. It is just unnerving; it is not making me physically ill."

"What does it feel like?" asked Khon'Tor.

"As if time is off. A step behind or ahead. As if

whatever is happening is catching up with what has already happened—like an echo. Perhaps I will adjust after a while. Please carry on; there is not much time before the High Council members arrive."

Acaraho turned to Khon'Tor and Awan. "If we wish to learn more about this system, it is going to require more than the four of us. With your permission Khon'Tor—".

Khon'Tor nodded.

"Awan—prepare two teams of guards. Have them bring the means to mark the tunnels as they go lest they get lost. We need to know as much as possible about Kthama Minor in the shortest amount of time. They must be cautious because we have no idea what lies in the lower areas. There could be settling in places, even cave-ins. We must get an idea of the size of this place— how many levels, if there are larger spaces below, living quarters, and so on. Any knowledge they return with will be more than we know now. It feels humid farther down the tunnel; as Haan said, the Mother Stream also runs through this section, but where does it go? Is there a path next to it, as there is under Kthama?"

Awan nodded.

"Under no circumstances are they to enter the Wall of Records, and they must disturb as little as possible everywhere else," he continued.

"Acaraho and Adia, what did you find in that large tunnel?" asked Khon'Tor.

"It has several forks and not too far down there appears to be a chamber. We could not enter; a huge rock seals it off," said Acaraho.

"Haan, do you know anything about another sealed chamber within Kthama Minor?

"No, I do not. Only that the Mothoc sealed Kthama Minor itself."

"The High Council members will be here very soon, and I think we first need to explore that chamber ourselves," said Acaraho.

"That is what I was afraid you were going to say, Commander." Khon'Tor said it as a joke, but there was an undercurrent of truth. Everyone was exhausted. Even Haan seemed no longer to stand as tall.

"How far down is it? Do we need Haan's help to open it?" he asked Acaraho.

"It is not far. As for opening it, we will know in a few moments."

Acaraho collected Adia, who was still leaning against the side wall. He steadied her as the four of them entered the tunnel to the left.

"Here it is." The High Protector took time for a closer look, feeling along the edges of the stone that blocked the doorway.

He froze.

"What is it?" asked Khon'Tor, the stress of recent events trying his patience. What do you think is behind it?"

"It may not be a question of *what,* Khon'Tor. It may be a question of *who.*"

"*What are you talking about*?" snapped Khon'Tor.

"The stone blocking the door, and the mudding along the edges? Both were done from the other side, Adoeete." Acaraho continued, "This chamber was sealed from the *inside.*"

CHAPTER 9

Khon'Tor ran his hand through the streak of white hair on his crown. He had heard what Acaraho said, but his mind was refusing to comprehend it. "Acaraho, it is late. We are all exhausted."

"The rock was placed from inside the chamber. The mudding around the cracks was then put in place, packed into the cracks from the inside. Whoever went in there sealed the chamber once they were inside. And whoever went in there, unless there is another exit, entered willingly and planned on never coming out."

The five of them looked at each other. Haan loomed over them all, quietly standing as he waited for the next move. Oh'Dar stood to the back, feeling intimidated by the weight of what they were doing.

The others stepped out of the way, and Haan, taking his cue, stepped forward and placed his hands on the large boulder. He squared his feet and pushed against the rock. As the seal broke, pieces cracked loose, chips, and little flakes coming off all around the edges on the inside. When it was finally free from the mudded ring, Haan slid the rock smoothly into the chamber.

It was pitch black inside. And eerie. The air around them seemed to go dead. Haan stooped and entered first, the dry air causing him to cough. Once inside, he stepped to the side so the others could join him. Khon'Tor first, then Awan, and Oh'Dar.

Acaraho reached back to help Adia through the doorway. He pulled her next to him and put an arm around her waist just in time to catch her before she fell.

"I am taking you back," he said.

"No, I need to see this. I *need to be here*," Adia insisted.

The air was stale and dry, and it took a moment for their eyes to adjust. The chamber was large and circular, and smooth walls stretched up to meet the high ceiling overhead.

Oh'Dar could not see much of anything and had stopped moving forward.

Adia and Acaraho followed Khon'Tor, only a few feet behind.

They could barely make out several large shapes against the walls, perhaps they were carvings, but no one could be sure.

As if on cue, their low-light vision kicked in. No

one said anything, but Acaraho's words hung in the air. He had been right. Whoever had entered had sealed it from the inside, never intending to leave.

There were three of them, close to the same size though one was slightly smaller, spaced evenly around the perimeter of the room.

Almost perfectly mummified and sealed in for thousands of years, sat three gigantic figures.

Adia looked at the one on the left. Her eyes started at floor level, then worked their way up, following the shape of the mammoth body. She could not have imagined anything this size. Haan and his people were huge, and these were nearly twice the size.

Their seats and armrests had been carved out of stone. Their feet were firmly planted on the ground, their bodies erect. Their hands dangled off the armrests. Were it not for the offset position of their heads in the darkened chamber, one might think they were still alive.

Khon'Tor could not take his eyes off the center figure. Instead of the dark brownish-black hair, similar to Haan's, of the two figures seated on either side, whoever was in the middle had what looked like silver hair over his entire body.

It took all of Khon'Tor's will to move closer; his body's instinctive response was to freeze. The figures were so well preserved that it felt as if any moment they would open their eyes and look down at him.

Now that the others had moved from the doorway, a crack of light had entered. It reached across the floor and threw enough illumination for Oh'Dar to see. He could not help himself and let out a gasp. He covered his mouth immediately, not wishing to cry out further.

The three figures were seated at three points of the chamber, equidistant from each other. On the wall over their heads, Khon'Tor could now see symbols carved into the rock.

He stared at the symbol above the silver-haired figure, and his mouth hung open.

Haan stepped forward and stood next to Khon'-Tor, looking up with reverence at the bodies. Then he surprised them all by kneeling.

"Moc'Tor. Father of the Mothoc. Father of the Wrak-Wavara. Father-Of-Us-All," he said, head bowed.

Tor? Khon'Tor thought—half statement half question.

The symbol carved into the wall above the silver beast was just what Khon'Tor had recognized it to be —the symbol of his father and his father before him, the mark of his bloodline. The pure mark of 'Tor.

Khon'Tor ran his hand through the silver in the crown of his hair. The same silver color as the hair that covered the last remains of Moc'Tor, Father-of-Us-All. He was looking at his direct ancestor. *I should have known; how did I never piece it together? All the stories Haan told about the Fathers, the Ancients, the Mothoc that lived at Kthama. I never made the connec-*

tion that I was a direct descendent of the Mothoc Leader. Khon'Tor could not take his eyes off of Moc'Tor. *His blood runs in my veins; he is my ancestor, Leader of the Ancients, who set in motion the inter-breeding with the Brothers.*

Haan was still kneeling, head bowed. They waited for him to finish showing his respect. After he rose, Khon'Tor asked quietly, "Do you know who the others are, Haan?"

The Sarnonn slowly looked from the silver-haired figure of Moc'Tor to the one on his right. It was a female, and she could only be one. "E'ranale. Beloved mate to Moc'Tor." He stepped toward the third, looked at the symbol above his head, and found the slight variation in the mark of the House of 'Tor. "This is Straf'Tor, brother to Moc'Tor. Leader of the rebellion that split our people into two branches, Sassen and Akassa."

They stood in silence for a while, now also overcome by a deep sense of reverence. These three had walked Etera thousands of years ago. Their decisions had created civil unrest and bloodshed and caused families to be divided forever. This was their legacy; this was the price which had bought the future, that of the People and the Sarnonn. But without it, none of them would now be standing here before what remained of the three Mothoc Leaders.

Oh'Dar moved to stand beside his mother, who was still supported by Acaraho.

"There are more markings," said Awan, pointing higher above the heads of the three figures.

Toward the top of the chamber, scrolling above the symbols of the bloodline was a long line of other symbols carved into the stone. Not organized like the markings in the Wall of Records, this looked very much like a message.

"Can anyone make them out?" asked Khon'Tor.

"They are too high up, and it is too dark near the top," said Awan.

"We are going to have to come back with torches. I hate to do it, but we need to know what it says. Haan, would you be able to tell us what the carvings mean?" asked Khon'Tor.

Haan nodded. Though he was far taller than the People and his low-light vision more developed, it was still too dark for even him to make out the symbols.

Acaraho was still supporting Adia, who was now losing strength rapidly.

"Khon'Tor, I have to get her out of here," he said, picking his mate up to carry her out.

"Let us all go; we need some time to deal with this," Khon'Tor agreed.

As Acaraho turned back toward the chamber opening, still holding Adia, she glanced up.

"Wait. Wait. What is that?" she asked, seeing a marking over the doorway.

"It is a drawing, I think," said Oh'Dar, moving toward it and squinting.

He became very silent. The memory of an old story his mother had recently told him burned through his mind.

"It is a picture drawn on the wall," said Acaraho. It is a bird. A blue bird." Squinting, he added, "a blue bird with a red berry in its mouth. Or a red stone."

"Mama," said Oh'Dar.

Adia fought to stay conscious, but could no longer and went limp in Acaraho's arms.

They made their way outside as quickly as possible. The fresh air was a welcome shock to them all. Acaraho carried Adia as gently as he could, taking her directly to the Healer's Quarters while Awan went to find Nadiwani.

Acaraho laid Adia on the mat and arranged her as comfortably as he could. He sat down next to her, holding her hand and smoothing the hair away from her forehead. He stared at her, his heart pounding with fear, willing her to wake up. Each second was excruciating, waiting for Nadiwani to arrive.

Finally, she burst into the room. "What happened?"

"Adia was weak to begin with; she said she felt out of phase with the rest of the world. Then she collapsed. She insisted on staying; she said she had to be there," Acaraho said, filled with regret that he had listened to his mate. *She is so determined. It was either argue with her and upset her more, or give in to her wishes. Either way, I failed.*

"Bring me to her," a voice said from the other side of the room.

Acaraho startled; he had forgotten that Urilla Wuti was still there, recovering. He stood up and helped her over to sit beside Adia.

Putting her hand on Adia's forehead, Urilla Wuti closed her eyes. "She is far, far away. But not so far that she cannot get back. Let her rest. Keep her warm. She was born for this, Commander. You cannot keep her from her destiny."

Acaraho hated every word that Urilla Wuti was saying. *I do not want her to be born for this. I want her safe, with me, raising our offspring. What good is a duty, a cause, if it costs you everything you are fighting to protect?* "Tell me what to do," he said, feeling more frightened than he wanted to admit.

"Stay with her, Commander. Be here when she returns. She will want to know that you were here the whole time, loving and protecting her as always."

Return from where? She makes it sound like Adia is conscious somewhere else. That only her body is left behind. But I will do whatever Urilla Wuti says, anything to help her.

Adia was standing in the familiar alcove in the Corridor. But instead of the usual flowers, sunlight, and birdsong, it was quiet and dark. Twilight had just fallen, and bright stars were starting to twinkle overhead. Faint melodic tones seemed to accompany their winking in and out. As with everything there, it was far richer and deeper and more vibrant than could be explained. And always that familiar Presence, like an undercurrent almost below the threshold of perception—the one permeating everything, the one telling her she was safe, that all was as it should be.

She squinted into the growing darkness. Swirling mists were forming, and from out of them stepped a figure. Taller than she could have imagined, Adia had to tip her head back to see its face. Deep-set eyes and a strong brow. The body was fully covered in hair or fur—something. She should have been frightened, but she was not.

"I am E'ranale," the figure said. "I am the mate of Moc'Tor, the one whom the Sassen call the Father-Of-Us-All."

"I am Adia, Healer of the High Rocks," said Adia haltingly. She understood why Haan had knelt, and she gave in to an overpowering drive to do so herself.

"Rise, Adia," said E'ranale. "Do not be afraid, Healer of the High Rocks. Everything is happening as it should. These events were foreseen in the age of the Ancients. Trust yourself. No matter what, trust that you are guided and protected."

"Did you bring me here?" Adia asked. The towering giant chuckled, revealing huge, white piercing canines.

"I have been trying to bring you here since Haan

and his followers started the preparation ritual to open Kthama Minor. But you are strong. You have valiantly fought my pull," and she smiled again, "though you have felt ill because of your resistance."

If Adia had not been in this place, she would have found the Mothoc female's smile terrifying. But here it was a show of kindness and friendship. Of fellowship.

"What of Urilla Wuti? She has also been ill."

"You and Urilla Wuti are connected in ways you do not yet understand. Urilla Wuti is feeling better now, as will you when you return—now that you have surrendered to my call."

"The bird. The blue bird, the picture of the blue bird with the red berry in its mouth—that is when I found myself here," Adia said.

"Yes. But it is not a red berry, Healer of the High Rocks. It is a red stone. Red jasper. But you know this, even if you are not ready to face it."

"My mother's dream. The night before I was born, she dreamed that a blue bird visited her and dropped a piece of red jasper at her feet."

"The bird said that her daughter would be a great blessing to the People and that she would also bring another great blessing who should be named Oh'Dar," said E'ranale, completing the story.

Adia looked at the giant Mothoc female standing in front of her, only now seeing the shimmering iridescent quality to her hair covering. It was almost as if each hair was alive and dancing.

"You sent the dream?"

"The Great Spirit sent the dream, little one."

"Why did my mother have to die? I needed her," Adia said quietly, overcome with emotion.

"We all have questions about the hardships that life brings. We wonder why it is, if the Great Spirit loves us so, that we cannot learn without suffering. You and I will have many conversations yet, about your realm and this one, but they are not for this visit."

Adia's mouth hung open. *Am I going to be brought back here to speak with her again?*

"I know you have a thousand questions. Some of them I will answer, some of them I will not. But for now, our visit has achieved its purpose, and you need to return to Etera."

"Yes, our world, our existence."

"What you think of as reality. The vibration in which we live our lives in the body. Everything you experience in your world, the trees, rivers, animals, clouds, others—all exist on that plane. But there are many vibrations; where we are now is one of them. Your resistance to my pulling you here was what caused you to feel sick. Phasing between the different vibrations is unnerving, and resisting makes it worse. But now that you know when I am calling you, you can prepare, making sure your body is left safe while you are away from it."

The feelings hit Adia the hardest when she was already lying down, or while others were with her.

She wondered if that were so her physical body would be cared for while she was not in it.

She could not help but frown; she did not comprehend everything the Mothoc was saying—and desperately wanted to.

"I do not understand; what is a *vibration*?"

"You have a wolf living among you—Kweeuu. Have you not seen him tilt his head and prick his ears, hearing something when you hear nothing?"

Adia nodded.

"He hears something beyond what you can hear. You cannot pick it up, but he can. It does not exist for you because it is occurring in a way you are not built to register. But that does not make it any less real.

"You have felt the earth under you shudder at times. That is similar to a vibration—a speed at which something is shifting. Everything in creation is in motion. The life current is always forming, un-forming, re-forming according to divine pattern. But you are not aware of it because it is outside of your perception.

"Just as the tone that Kweeuu hears is beyond your ability to hear, to experience this place is beyond most people's ability until they return to the Mother. When you come here, you are shifting your vibration so you can experience life on this plane without your physical body having to perish. That is the clearest explanation I can give.

Then E'ranale continued, "You have probably

noticed your seventh sense abilities have been becoming more sensitive?"

"Yes. I seem to sense everything much more readily, more deeply."

"That progression will continue. When the Sarnonn Leader came to Kthama, he set in motion the movement toward the Age of Shadows. And when Kthama Minor was opened, great power was awakened. A power that has been waiting for a very long time. You remember the white light that shot up from the meadow above when the Sarnonn broke the seal of the Healer's stone?"

"Yes. It seemed to go right through me. And after that, my seventh sense seemed to become even more sensitive. And the feelings of being out of phase started."

"In time, you will learn to use your awakened abilities. Be patient."

Adia was concentrating so hard on everything E'ranale was telling her, but at the same time could not take her eyes off the Mothoc's hair covering. Everything in the Corridor seemed alive and pulsating, but her coat was even more mesmerizing as it shimmered and shifted. Adia took a step forward, reaching out to touch her. In a split second, E'ranale was no longer a few feet from Adia, but now a fair distance away.

Adia froze, color rising at her impudence.

"May I speak of this to the others?" she asked.

"They will learn in their own time. Trust the

current of life, which brings each of us to what we need at the appointed time. For now, this experience is between you and me. You may discuss it with Urilla Wuti, but no one else. As for the High Protector, because he is your mate, you may tell him that you had a conversation with me, and you may give him my assurance that things are unfolding as they should, but do not disclose details of our conversation at this time."

Silence fell for what felt like a moment, and then a lifetime.

"Create your intention to return, Adia. Urilla Wuti prepared you to be ready for this point. Now the next level of your training has just begun. You may seek me if you wish, but I may not always answer. Trust that this, too, is as it should be."

Adia took one last long look at the Mothoc giant, trying to memorize every detail. Then she closed her eyes, took a deep breath, and willed herself to return to what she still thought of as reality.

She opened her eyes to see Acaraho sitting beside her. It was as if all the color had been drained from the world. It was flat and bland, a pale echo of where she had just come from. *Each time I am there, it is more and more of a shock to return.*

Acaraho saw Adia's eyes open.

"You are awake. Are you alright? You passed out in the chamber at Kthama Minor," he said.

She reached up and wrapped her arms around his neck, and he pulled her gently to him. Urilla

Wuti was lying down on the mat next to Adia, but now she sat up and put her hand on Adia's shoulder. Nadiwani came over from where she was working at the preparation table.

"Are you feeling better?" asked Urilla Wuti.

"Yes, I am—and you?"

"Yes. Much."

Adia realized that Urilla Wuti must have had a similar experience and that it was as the Mothoc had said; they would both feel better now.

"What have I missed?" Adia asked.

"Nothing, really," Acaraho reassured her. "We all came back after you passed out. We want to go back in, before the High Council arrives, and have Haan try to read the markings above the bodies."

"Bodies?" said Urilla Wuti.

"You must come with us this time," said Acaraho. "You also need to see it. I will carry you if need be."

Urilla Wuti shifted in her place. "I do not like being carried, Commander. It makes me feel old and frail. Though the experience itself is quite pleasant," she added almost absentmindedly.

"It is an honor to be of service to you, Urilla Wuti. You must receive it in that spirit," he said. "Giving and receiving is the breath of love, and if you are not open to receiving, others are denied the gift of giving."

"How did you get so smart, Commander?" she joked.

"I do not know about that, but I have my

moments. The smartest thing I ever did was pairing with the Healer here," he said. "The rest I am not so sure about."

"When are we going back in?" Adia asked.

"Everyone needs rest; it was an overwhelming experience. Probably not until tomorrow, and we must hope that the High Council does not arrive before we are finished. We need some time to examine that chamber more closely on our own. Awan's group is probably already on its way there."

"It feels wrong to be in there. With the Ancients," said Adia softly.

"I feel the same. Perhaps when this is over, it should be resealed."

"That is how I feel. It is, after all, a burial vault."

"It is getting late. We should all eat and then retire. I was just preparing something," said Nadiwani. "Urilla Wuti and I have many questions for tomorrow."

Everyone agreed, and afterward, Nadiwani returned to her quarters, taking Urilla Wuti with her. Acaraho and Adia decided to spend the night in the Healer's Quarters.

Acaraho lay next to Adia, and she cuddled up against him, her head on his chest. His strong heartbeat and the warmth of him were comforting. She tried to move in tighter, and he helped her by wrapping his arms around her.

He kissed Adia on the top of her head. "Are you alright, Saraste'? Please tell me what is going on?"

She always melted when he used the term of endearment.

"I feel much better now. The sick feeling, it was one of them trying to connect with me."

"One of *them*? *Them* them? Surely you do not mean one of the dead Mothoc in the chamber we just left? Who have been closed up there for eons?"

"Yes. One of *them* them. It was E'ranale, the female, mate to Moc'Tor."

He let out a huge sigh. "I would never doubt you, Healer. I have experienced things myself that I would not have believed possible. But I don't have to understand everything, as long as you are alright. That is all that matters. But is there anything I need to know about this contact she made with you?" Acaraho was remembering their lovemating in the Dream World before they were able to be paired at the last Ashwea Awhidi. He knew from direct experience that there were other realities than the one they knew.

"She mostly reassured me that things were unfolding as they should. And she said that now we had made contact, I would feel better. And she was right. The dizziness and shifting sensation is gone. And for that, I am very grateful."

"I will not pry, but you know you can tell me anything. Let us get some sleep. Tomorrow the High

Council members will arrive, and I would like to have Haan interpret the message in that chamber before they do. We have some long days ahead, and I want you rested and well." He did not ask about their offspring, though what effect this might be having was heavy on his mind.

He pulled the covers up over them both. Adia turned over, and Acaraho slid up behind her, his arm wrapped around her waist and his nose happily buried in the sweet lavender scent of her hair.

"She is strong," said E'ranale. "Our visions were correct. She will help them find their way through this. And the one named Oh'Dar will continue to prove his value to them. As for the offling she carries—their offling—now is not the time to burden her with that. I will speak with her later, after the hardest of this is passed."

CHAPTER 10

O h'Dar awoke next to Nootau in Nadiwani's quarters. Though they were no longer youngsters, both still enjoyed the comfort and sense of belonging in sleeping over with her. This morning Urilla Wuti was there as well. His thoughts immediately turned to Acise. *I pray she is alright. I know that Is'Taqa and Honovi will make sure Pajackok does not bother her. But I will feel better when we are together again. With all this going on, when will we be able to be paired?*

Mating. Ben explained it to me. But I wonder if I could still go through an Ashwea Tare. I am sure that whatever pleases our females would please her. I want to make her so happy that she will forgive me for leaving her and never think of it again. Perhaps I will also make her a necklace similar to the one Khon'Tor had me make for Tehya. Oh'Dar suddenly realized that he had never given out all the gifts. Well, there would be time for that later. At some point, things had to settle down.

He rose and quietly nosed around the food area, careful not to wake the others. Not immediately finding anything he wanted, he slipped out and went to look for his parents.

Acaraho, Adia, Khon'Tor, and Tehya were seated in the Great Chamber. Oh'Dar joined them, sitting next to Khon'Tor.

"The High Council members should arrive today. I, for one, would like to find out ahead of their arrival what that message says," said Acaraho.

"I agree. You mentioned torches," said Khon'Tor.

"Yes. I hate to risk it, with the Mothoc being so— dry," he stumbled at not finding a better word.

Even Khon'Tor had to smile at that, shaking his head. "*Dry* is as good a word as any, and I share your concern."

"What about the fluorite?" Oh'Dar suggested. "If someone has a larger piece that is charged already, it might provide enough glow for Haan to see by."

Acaraho nodded. "I wonder who might have a large piece. All those I know of are smaller."

"There is one in our quarters," said Tehya. "It was brought in when the females decorated it for us. It is over in the corner, next to your Leader's Staff, Adoeete. There is a shaft of light over that corner. It was glowing last night, so we would need to wait for it to recharge this morning."

"I am going to find something to write on—I assume I am going back in with you?" asked Oh'Dar.

"Yes. What do you mean, *write on*?" asked Khon'Tor.

"I mentioned it before. It is something I learned from the Waschini—a detailed marking system. It is similar to how we make markings. If Haan can tell us what the symbols mean, I can mark that down in the Waschini language. Then, later, I can use that to speak exactly what it said. It is more precise than our simple markings and can be understood by others with virtually no loss in meaning."

Khon'Tor thought a moment.

"Oh'Dar. Could you teach our offspring to *write*?"

The thought had not occurred to Oh'Dar, but he remembered how Miss Blain had taught him.

"I believe I could. We would have to collect some materials and make some adaptations, but yes, I think I could."

Acaraho and Adia looked at each other, and Adia smiled. Both were proud of their son.

Khon'Tor said, "Do not forget about this. After everything settles down, you must implement it. It does not matter if it is Waschini markings or not—if their way of making scratches for others to understand later is more detailed, more accurate, then the offspring should learn how to do it.

"Perhaps we all should, young or old," he added.

"We need a more reliable means than memory. Handing stories down from generation to generation has proven to be a failure in some respects."

"I will remember, Khon'Tor," promised Oh'Dar. "But there may be no way to separate the writing from the language. What you are asking me to do means I must also teach them Whitespeak."

Khon'Tor stared at Oh'Dar for a moment.

"Also, my lifespan is shorter than those of the People. Someone would have to come after me to keep it going."

The Leader nodded. "Thank you for speaking up. If our offspring have to learn Whitespeak so they can record and use the markings, then so be it."

"If we are going back in, Urilla Wuti should come with us," Adia suggested. "I believe she is up to it now. And perhaps also Tehya. Once the High Council arrives, we will have little undisturbed time to take it in."

"Nadiwani too. We should all go. You are right," agreed Khon'Tor.

He rose from the bench. "I am going to retrieve the fluorite. Tehya, would you like to stay here?"

"I will come with you. I would like to put on something warmer if we are going into a cavern that has been closed up for thousands of years. You can help me pick it out," she teased.

"Maybe I should come with you to help," joked Adia. "I would not want you two to get sidetracked and be late."

Khon'Tor gave a wicked smile. "I promise you; we will not be long."

Tehya wrapped her fingers around his hand and tugged. "Come on. We have to check on Arismae beforehand too, and make sure Mapiya can keep her until I return."

Everyone scattered—Oh'Dar to find something to write with and write on, and Acaraho to look for Awan and send a messenger to fetch Haan. Adia went to find Nadiwani and Urilla Wuti.

Before long, they were reassembled in the Great Entrance. Khon'Tor did not remember ever having seen Tehya so covered up, though he had enjoyed watching her dress.

Awan arrived with Haan, and they were ready. The past few days had been sunny, though everyone had been so preoccupied they had hardly realized. But Adia did notice that the plants along the path to Kthama Minor had sprung up very quickly, poking through the last dusting of snow. Some of them were already about to bloom. She glanced out past those on the immediate path and realized that nowhere else was there such an early profusion of growth. Urilla Wuti had also noticed the sudden development, and Adia looked back and caught her eye.

When they arrived at the Healer's Cove, the vines the Sarnonn had torn down when they separated the huge stone from the rock wall were already growing back.

This is not normal, Adia thought to herself. *We are barely approaching spring.*

They entered Kthama Minor and made their way to the sacred chamber. Khon'Tor insisted on leading Tehya by the hand, not taking a chance of her being separated from them in the network of tunnels.

Haan stepped through the opening first, holding the largest fluorite rock they could find. As before, it took a moment for their eyesight to catch up with the change in light, though the glow from the fluorite did dispel some of the shadows. He moved over to the far wall where the markings were inscribed above the seated figures.

Urilla Wuti stood in awe. There were no words for the significance of the place in which they were standing. Even aside from the sacredness of the chamber they had entered, no one could be prepared for the size of the Mothoc. It did explain why the corridors and rooms of Kthama were so large, far bigger than the People needed. Whereas Urilla Wuti believed the People might in time adjust to the size of the Sarnonn, there was no way she could imagine they would ever have been able to walk among these beasts without living on constant alert.

Her eyes adapted, and she looked more closely at the silver-haired figure.

Acaraho said in hushed and reverent tones, "That is Moc'Tor. The one whom Haan calls the Father-Of-Us-All. It was he who led the Wrak-Wavara. The other is his mate, E'ranale, and the one farthest away is the brother to Moc'Tor. We do not know all the story yet, but that is what Haan said the first time we entered. These must be the Ancients."

Haan held up the fluorite stone as high as he could. The light it cast was enough to throw shadows on the markings carved into the wall—shadows which provided the relief and contrast necessary for him to make them out.

Oh'Dar stood ready with his charcoal and birch bark.

The message carved by the Ancients into the high wall had waited thousands of years to be discovered.

Welcome, our Beloveds. We have waited for you. Now that you realize your need for each other, may you join to create the future of your making. May the sounds of your offling fill the halls of Kthama forever. The guidance you need will come through Kthama's Healer.

Haan took a moment to go over it, wanting to make sure he understood correctly. Finally, he said, "The writings give a welcome and call us their loved ones. It says they have waited for us, and now that we realize our need for each other, we are called to join together to create the future of our making. That phrase I am certain about, I have heard it before. Then it says may the sounds of our offling echo through Kthama once again and continue on. Lastly, that the help we need will come from Kthama's Healer."

Haan lowered the glowing rock and stepped away

from the wall. Oh'Dar finished writing, and everyone stood for a moment, taking in the message.

"They knew we could not be here reading this if the Sarnonn and Akassa had not found a way to work together," said Khon'Tor. "But why forbid you to contact us, yet make it impossible for us to open Kthama Minor without your ability to enter into the Ror'Eckrah?" he asked Haan.

"The separation between our people was bitter. Perhaps it was intended to keep us apart until the Sassen's anger at the Akassa had faded. Clearly, from this, the Mothoc believed that at some point, we would come together. But maybe that point depended on a shift in our thinking. The Fathers did not want our blood diluted further with the Others'. And you were not safe from us—still are not safe from all of us. But there were enough of us who recognized the need for our tribes to come back together that we were able to open Kthama Minor."

"It appears it was their plan all along—that, in time, we would find each other," said Khon'Tor.

"Their plan, or at least their hope," said Nadi-wani, finally coming out of the same paralyzing sense of awe that Urilla Wuti was feeling.

"*Look for help to come through your Healer*," repeated Khon'Tor. He turned to Adia, who was looking a little pale.

She was afraid she knew what it meant, and prayed that she was up to the responsibility. *I do not have the answers; I do not know how to move forward.*

Then Adia remembered E'ranale's assurances that she would be guided and protected.

"We need to get back," said Acaraho, eyeing his mate. "I suggest we close the chamber as soon as possible. They have survived for thousands of years, but most likely only because it was sealed off from the damp air coming up from the Mother Stream."

As they turned to leave, the fluorite cast light onto the floor next to Straf'Tor. A bundle of dried reeds, interwoven, lay at his feet.

Oh'Dar looked closer. "This looks like what is left of a basket of some type. I wonder what it held?"

"Perhaps the mud to fill the cracks around the rock that sealed the chamber," suggested Acaraho.

One by one, they stepped out, Adia and Oh'Dar pausing to take one last look at the picture over the entrance of the blue bird with the red stone in its beak.

So I will somehow be instrumental in whatever is to happen, Adia thought. Urilla Wuti sensed Adia's concern and took her hand.

Haan pulled the rock back in place as tightly as he could. Then the entourage made its way back to Kthama. As they walked back, Adia looked once again at the profusion of life blooming along the pathway that ran between the two cave systems.

Haan went on his way, and as the others reached Kthama, one of the watchers informed Acaraho and First Guard Awan that the High Council members were almost there. Acaraho had Awan send a contingent down to the Mother Stream to greet them and escort them to their quarters, with a message to meet at the evening meal after the travelers had rested. It was a long journey, and he knew they would be tired and probably hungry.

After Awan had been dispatched, Acaraho turned back to the group. "Well, it has begun. When do you want to convene the council, Khon'Tor? And do you wish Haan to join it when it starts, or later?"

"I would prefer to start it without him. Depending on the searchers' reports on the structure of Kthama Minor and before approaching Haan about it, I want to inform them I am allowing Haan's following to move there. I would prefer to have their agreement, though I would move ahead without it. If there is dissension, I would rather Haan not be present for it."

"I have a report for you on Kthama Minor," answered Acaraho. "There are at least four levels, and there is a great stream running through the lowest level, just as in Kthama. However, it is lower than the Mother Stream, and we are not sure if it is the same source or if there is a second underground river. At present, we have no way to tell. There are a variety of living areas, some larger and some smaller. There is evidence that food preparation and storage was also part of their community. So far, we have found no ventilation shafts, so the air does not move as freely as it does here. That would be the first improvement to make. The second would be creating markings for the tunnels until they become familiar. We did not follow each one; there are too many. But, with time, they could be investigated."

"Is it secure?" asked Khon'Tor.

"There is no evidence of cave-ins, no sinkholes, and all the walls are smooth with no cracks or other damage. As best we can tell, it is stable."

"Any other water sources?"

"Nothing like we have here. Oh, no, wait; we came across several small pools. They could have been used for bathing, or waste removal—it is hard to tell. Otherwise, no."

"Realizing that the guards did not have time to make a full check of everything, is there any evidence of any connection, opening, closed or otherwise, between there and Kthama?" Khon'Tor asked.

"No. And they specifically looked. They checked everywhere on the adjoining walls that they could. If there is one, it is well hidden."

"Very well," said Khon'Tor. "I do not expect trouble from Haan's people, but if there were a secret way into Kthama from Kthama Minor, we would be best to know about it before offering it to him."

They all nodded. Acaraho offered his opinion. "Let us meet with the High Council members first thing in the morning. We can describe the events to this point, and no doubt they will be anxious to see Kthama Minor, at which time we should involve Haan."

"I agree. Until tomorrow morning after first meal, then," said Khon'Tor.

When Khon'Tor and Tehya were almost at their quarters, he scooped her up and gently threw her over his shoulder, to which she laughed and squealed with delight.

He kicked the wooden door, almost shattering it, and carried her over to the chair that Oh'Dar had made. He plopped her down unceremoniously, which also made her smile as she sank into the over-sized, over-stuffed creation.

He kneeled in front of her and stopped. "It has been too long. How do you get out of this thing? I want it off."

She smiled and sat up, "Let me go put something else on."

"No."

Her eyes widened. Usually, she had some covering, even if it was conveniently moved out of the way. Her face reddened at the thought of being so exposed to him. She looked over at the light shaft and realized the sun was setting—but it was still too light. "Adoeete, then let us talk awhile. It is not yet dark,"

"No."

Her heart beat wildly in her chest.

"I want to see you. Remove this, or I will."

She knew that their love play often went along these lines. She secretly loved it when he told her what to do, but in this case, she was embarrassed.

"Can we negotiate?"

"I am not in the mood to negotiate."

"Well, I am in the mood. I will take this off if I can have the bed cover. What if I get cold?"

He looked at her. "It is a reasonable request. Though we both know the reason for your request is not that you will get cold."

Then he added, "You are so beautiful, Tehya. It is a great pleasure for me to look upon you."

His softened approach melted her heart. She sat up and slipped the long buckskin off over her head. She heard him let out a long breath when at last, she was sitting in front of him with no barriers to his gaze.

He pulled her hips to him, causing her to slide down on the softsit, as she had named it.

He leaned over her and kissed her softly, letting his lips linger on hers. He then moved to her neck, tracing her collar bone slowly and lovingly. He moved lower and briefly took the pink tip of her pale mound in his mouth and gently swirled it with his tongue. Her moans of pleasure assured him that he was pleasing her. A moment longer and he drew his tongue down the front of her belly, making a slow wet path as he shifted his position. As he continued down her front, she sat up in alarm.

"Adoeete, stop."

"What is it, Tehya?" He looked up.

"Please. Please, that is far enough."

"You agreed to submit to me."

"Adoeete—"

"Did you or did you not give yourself to me?"

"Yes, no, please it is just—"

"Did you, *or did you not*, give yourself to me?" He locked her in his gaze.

"No, Adoeete—" she said quietly, color now blazing across her cheeks at what she thought he was about to do to her.

"No? That is not true. You belong to me, Tehya. And I to you. You will let me do to you as I wish," and he gently pushed her back down onto the softsit.

He slid down into a position between her legs, gently pushing apart her thighs. She instinctively tried to bring them together. Khon'Tor simply placed one hand on each and pushed them back apart.

If he had looked up, he would have seen her arm bent over her eyes to hide her shame at being so completely exposed.

"Please, no." Her cheeks burned, and she covered her face with both hands.

Gently, he pushed up the soft down covering her mound up and out of the way with his hand. He heard her inhale sharply. He increased pressure on her thighs to keep them apart. Touching her lightly, he made the same circles he had taught her to do to please herself. The scent of her incited his passion. He could hear her breathing deepen. He pressed his thumb against her entrance, and her desire for him flowed. He murmured, "I love looking at you," to which she turned her head, embarrassed by his words.

"Nooooo—" she protested, but he knew, regardless of her feelings of shame, that his administrations would please her greatly.

He continued until he felt her body tense and stiffen. She involuntarily raised herself to him as if to demand more. He increased his ardor and heard her catch her breath, then breathe even more deeply. He continued until he knew she was close and switched to an unchanging pattern. Finally, he felt her jerk, then freeze as ecstasy took her away from everything. Mad with the desire to drive himself into her, so wet and unguarded, it was all he could do to let her finish.

He waited for the spasms to stop, then moved over her and pressed himself against her. As his thick shaft separated her, he kissed her neck and whispered, "You are mine."

Tehya wrapped her legs and arms around him as far as she could, clasping him to her.

With the sight and smell of her still filling his senses, he rocked her small frame with each long stroke until he did not want to wait any longer, and he shot his hot stream deep inside her, his grinding hard against her causing her to spend again.

Tehya rolled over, exhausted and fully satisfied. Khon'Tor rose, gently lifted her, and carried her to their sleeping mat where he pulled up the covers to keep her warm. He whispered in her ear how enjoyable it had been for him and how much he loved her. Kweeuu came over from his mat, and Khon'Tor allowed it as it seemed to please his mate to be sandwiched between him and the fluffy grey wolf.

Tehya let out a sigh of relief, happiness, contentment. Khon'Tor expected that she would wake later, hungry, but for now, he let her drift off to sleep. He knew Mapiya would gladly keep Arismae as long as she could.

Khon'Tor sat for a while, watching Tehya sleep. Her long eyelashes were closed softly against her cheeks; her honey-gold hair was splayed across the mat. Finally, he lay down with her and gave himself over to sleep as well.

There was someone in the room. Someone was standing over her. She could not move. Her legs and hands were bound. In the corner was Arismae, helpless. He was there to finish what he had started. She struggled against the ties binding her, eyes wide as he moved toward Arismae's nest. Her worst fears were materializing in front of her; she tried to scream, but nothing came out. She froze and watched helplessly as the intruder bent over and picked Arismae up.

Khon'Tor awoke as Tehya bolted upright. "Oh no, oh no, he is here. He is here in the room. *Where is Arismae?*" She was hysterical, her arms flailing, and her eyes darting around the room.

Khon'Tor knelt in front of her, so she was forced to look at him.

"Listen to me. No one is here. Only me. And Kweeuu. There is no one else in the room, Tehya. You are safe; there is no one else here. *And there never will be.*"

Tehya started to shake, and Khon'Tor wrapped his arms around her. He put his hand on her head as she buried her face in his chest hair. He let her cry it out, his heart breaking that she had been terrorized so—and still was. Despite all his reassurances, the nightmares would not stop.

Khon'Tor remembered back to when he was so sick and too weak to be moved, and Haan had come to talk with him. Haan had brought Akar'Tor. Akar'Tor had been in their quarters. Again, he cursed himself for his bad judgment in ever allowing that.

Tehya calmed down as he rocked her gently.

Perhaps we need to move to other quarters. How can I assure Tehya that she is safe? But Khon'Tor knew the answer.

It was Khon'Tor's presence itself that was frightening her. Physically, they were too much alike; what had been a comfort to Tehya now only reminded her of the one who had stolen her sense of safety.

Khon'Tor had to find Akar'Tor, even if only what was left of him. And if by chance Akar'Tor was still alive, Khon'Tor had to bring back the physical proof —no matter how gruesome—that he was no longer a threat to Tehya or Arismae.

The next morning, while Tehya was sitting with the others, Khon'Tor left his meal to find Awan.

"A word with you, First Guard," he said, leading Awan out of earshot.

"I need a sparring partner. Someone well versed in spear work and the use of the staff."

"Does Acaraho know of this request, Adik'Tar?"

Khon'Tor stared at Awan.

"Am I no longer Leader?" he snapped out. "What business is this of the High Protector?"

"I meant no offense, Adik'Tar. It is, in fact, your position that requires me to notify High Protector Acaraho of your request. My allegiance is to you both. Should any harm come to you, and I had not told Acaraho ahead of time, I would be remiss in my duty to protect you. I have seen the High Protector when he is angered. I do not want to be the target of that, ever."

Khon'Tor sighed and placed his hand on Awan's shoulder.

"I understand. You may inform Acaraho, but no one else. And we can use flexible switches for practice, though they will still sting. I do not wish to inflict harm *or* be harmed myself, but I have not tested my skills for some time, and I feel a need to do so."

"I will make the arrangements. The size of your opponent?"

"Close to my size. Younger, if you have someone suitable and willing."

Awan knew what this was about. He knew it was tied to the weapon that Khon'Tor had commissioned him to make. And he knew who the real target of this skill-building practice would eventually be. "I hope you find him, Adik'Tar," he said as Khon'Tor walked away.

Khon'Tor turned and looked back. "I will."

CHAPTER 11

The inner circle of the High Council was assembled. Lesharo'Mok, Leader of the People of the Deep Valley, Harak'Sar, Leader of the People of the Far High Hills, Bidzel and Yuma'qia, the record keepers, and Kurak'Kahn, the High Council Overseer sat patiently waiting. With the exception of Awan, the members of Khon'Tor's Circle of Counsel were seated in a row to the side of the door.

The Overseer opened the meeting and turned the floor over to Khon'Tor.

"We have much to cover. But before I start, it is with great sadness that I must let you know that Ogima Adoeete, High Chief of the Brothers, has returned to the Great Spirit. He was a great ally to the People, and he was a great inspiration to me. His wisdom and leadership will be sorely missed. Is'Taqa has taken over as Chief of the Brothers."

Khon'Tor paused for a moment, as those in attendance bowed their heads and whispered in unison, "Safe passage, Chief Ogima Adoeete, until we meet again in the Great Spirit."

When he had their attention again, Khon'Tor said, "I asked you to return because Kthama Minor has been located and is accessible. Haan and a group of followers opened it several days ago."

No one said a word, so Khon'Tor continued.

"The opening ritual is difficult to explain. Suffice it to say; there is much to the Sarnonn of which we are not aware. They have abilities that we do not possess. I do not believe that even the most gifted of our Healers possesses anywhere near the level of their skills. The closest I can explain is that they seemed to be in some sort of trance, joined as one body with one intention. Haan called it the Ror'Eckrah; he was in the lead and seemed to be the only one with awareness as a separate self. They split into two groups, and between them broke the seal on the stone that was hiding the entrance to Kthama Minor. My words fail in trying to convey the experience. There is a great deal to the Sarnonn of which we are ignorant."

"Inside and down one of the main tunnels is a large room, though *large* does not do it justice. The walls are covered with markings, and I am hoping that our record keepers will be able to make sense of it. Haan called it the Wall of Records. It is best you see for yourselves."

Bidzel and Yuma'qia sat up straighter and turned quickly to each other. "When may we see this?" they interrupted, almost in unison.

Khon'Tor let the lapse in protocol go; this was the most significant discovery in their history, and everyone would have to demonstrate forbearance. "As soon as the Overseer decides it is time. We only entered it once and only went a few steps in. We felt we were on holy ground and did not wish to disturb anything further. There is more. But you must also see that for yourselves. I will not even attempt to describe it."

The council members were glancing at each other, with no idea of what lay ahead.

Khon'Tor spoke again. "Both of the Healers, Adia and Urilla Wuti—who is still here with us from the Far High Hills—were deeply affected by the rituals of Haan and his followers. It is only now that they are feeling any relief."

Kurak'Kahn stood up. "Khon'Tor, you keep using the phrase *Haan and his followers*. Why not *Haan and his people*?"

"The distinction is accurate, Overseer. Haan's people have been splintered, much as what occurred ages ago during the Wrak-Wavara. He has only a small group that is willing to help us and receive our help in return. Because they joined us, they have been exiled from their home cave system of Kayerm. They are currently homeless."

"Where are they living now?"

"They are living in one of the meadows above Kthama," Khon'Tor said, and paused. "I have given this much thought, Overseer, and discussed it with those from whom I seek counsel. I have decided to allow Haan and his followers to move into Kthama Minor once we have finished our exploration. Of course, we would want access to the Wall of Records and any other finds of historical significance."

To his credit, Kurak'Kahn did not overstep his position. "It is your decision, Khon'Tor," he said. "For what it is worth, I believe it has merit."

"What of those who remain at Kayerm? Are they a threat?" asked Lesharo'Mok.

"They most certainly could be," Khon'Tor answered. "That was another consideration in allowing Haan's Sarnonn to occupy Kthama Minor. The others could take whatever they want, including Kthama. Having Haan's followers as allies can only help us should the dissidents decide not to keep to themselves."

"Has Haan accepted your offer?" asked Harak'Sar.

"I have not extended it," said Khon'Tor. "I planned to after you had a chance to see what we discovered."

"We are ready when you are," said Kurak'Kahn, speaking also for the others.

"I will send for Haan, and we will meet at the Great Entrance," said Khon'Tor.

Haan was in the meadow with his people when one of the watchers came to fetch him. The watcher looked around, not quite believing the proliferation of spring growth he was seeing, but said nothing, only telling Haan that the High Council members would like him to join them as they entered Kthama Minor.

Before long, the group was making its way toward what had been known as the Healer's Cove.

It still left Adia with a sense of awe that the entrance to Kthama Minor had been hidden for generations behind the great rock that had always held so much mystery for her.

Once again, she marveled at the sprouting of the plants, underbrush, and wildflowers along the way. She had meant to mention it to Urilla Wuti, but in all the commotion, it had slipped her mind. She had a theory and wanted to explore it at her earliest convenience. She would have to ask Acaraho to accompany her, as he would be concerned if she investigated it on her own.

The High Council members stood in front of the giant rock that had sealed Kthama Minor for thousands of years. They said nothing, their eyes running up and down, taking in the size, and imagining the strength needed to move a boulder of such bulk and weight.

Haan stepped forward and motioned them inside. Khon'Tor led the way, the High Council members behind him and the others following behind. The High Council members stopped and looked up, estimating the height of the ceilings. Comparable to Kthama, Kthama Minor was indeed made of the same caverns buried deep into the mountainside. Their feet disturbed the thin layer of debris that had accumulated untouched until a few days before.

Khon'Tor let them get their bearings, and gave them time for their eyes to adjust before motioning them on.

Haan knew that Khon'Tor wanted them to see the Wall of Records, but he would not show them the once-sealed burial chamber without leave from the Leader.

Khon'Tor led them down the winding tunnel to the Wall of Records, and the area became lighter the closer they got to the chamber. As before, sunlight filtered in through an opening in the top, washing the interior in a warm golden glow. Barely able to contain their excitement, Bidzel and Yuma'qia chattered together as they walked. When they stepped into the room, their eyes widened as they took in the wonder of the walls. Everywhere they looked, markings stretched from the bottom of the walls to the top and spilled onto the ceiling in places. At first, it appeared haphazard, but they began to collect themselves and look properly at what was in front of them.

"There is structure here. There is a pattern. This has meaning," said Bidzel, pointing to several places. Yuma'qia nodded in agreement.

The record keepers turned to Khon'Tor for permission to enter. He nodded, and they stepped in slowly and gingerly.

They started to the left of the opening, where they believed the first marks might have been placed. They studied what appeared to be different branches of symbols, with starts and stops as they spread out, like a web.

After a few moments, Yuma'qia spoke.

"Much of this looks to be a record of pairings. We are looking at perhaps the entire bloodline record of the Wrak-Wavara."

No one moved. No one breathed. The weight of the moment seemed to sink through them to the floor, cementing them in place. Not being able to find words worthy of the moment, they all stood in silence, waiting for the two record keepers to continue.

Bidzel took another step. He whispered to Yuma'qia and pointed, then took several steps farther, again whispering and pointing.

"Without rushing your examination, is there anything else you can tell us at this moment?" asked Khon'Tor. Bidzel and Yuma'qia continued whispering and pointing, shaking their heads and nodding at each other. After a few moments, Bidzel motioned for Khon'Tor to join them.

Pointing to one of the markings, he said, "We recognize many of the symbols. Here, do you recognize this one? Here. And here. This is the mark of Moc'Tor, and it is your family mark, Khon'Tor. They are identical; they have no variations. You are his direct descendant."

Khon'Tor did not mention the sealed chamber, or that he had already surmised this.

"And this here, this is his brother's, Straf'Tor. There is division here. Great division. If I am correct, these were the two factions that split during Wrak-Wavara. One of them continued breeding with the Brothers and became us, the People. The other, those under Straf'Tor, stopped their crossbreeding with the Brothers earlier than that. Here. But this is also the mark of 'Tor, though slightly modified. There is an extra qerl here, showing they are brothers of the same house."

"This mark next to Moc'Tor's symbol, it is missing from his brother's mark. But it appears again here, under one of Moc'Tor's offspring."

"That is the mark of the Guardian," explained Haan. "Moc'Tor was a Guardian. His brother Straf'Tor was not."

The record keepers followed the markings, which covered the walls up to and partly across the ceiling, never touching them but tracing them as closely as possible.

"We will need to build some type of climbing system to examine all of this. It is going to take a while, Overseer," said Bidzel, turning to face Kurak'Kahn.

"The amount of material here is staggering," he added. "It will take us years to figure it out. This is the missing information. Our records only go back several generations. This— This is the foundation of the separation of bloodlines. And there is no telling what other information might be recorded here that may help us solve the problems of our dwindling selection of safe pairings."

And perhaps the secret of how the giant Mothoc managed to interbreed with the much smaller Brothers, for one thing, thought Adia.

Bidzel turned back to the markings.

"Moc'Tor had several mates, but at some point, he chose to have only one. This is her mark here."

Yuma'qia was still studying Straf'Tor's line. It stretched too high for him to see everything, but he could still make out much of it. He followed the primary marks, then stopped cold. He turned and looked at Haan.

"You are directly of Straf'Tor's line."

Khon'Tor's head turned quickly at what Yuma'qia was saying.

"Yes," said Haan, turning to Khon'Tor, who was staring at him blankly. "I am 'Tor."

Were Haan's ancestors and mine then brothers? Are we related, both of the House of 'Tor? He said in the beginning that his parent's parents were at Kthama, so he has a right to be here, and this seals it. "You knew?" asked Khon'Tor.

"I have always known, brother," replied Haan, using the term loosely to honor their shared heritage.

"Akar'Tor was not named after you, Khon'Tor. I gave Akar the name of *my* house."

Akar'Tor. In my arrogance, I assumed Hakani had named him after me. In all this time, Haan never called himself Haan'Tor. And I thought nothing of it, thinking that in their culture they did not use bloodline names.

"Our people are not as diverse as yours," Haan added, sensing Khon'Tor's confusion. "There are only a few primary houses at Kayerm; most are of Straf'Tor's line or that of the Healer. Which has brought us to our current problem with not enough diversity in our bloodlines."

"The Healers?" asked Adia. "The Healers of your people can pair and have offspring?"

"Yes. The Healer's bloodline must not be broken. Other than the Guardians, his line carries the strongest Aezaitera, the connective force of the Great Spirit."

Guardians, Aezaitera. And yes, their healers are male. Adia shook her head. "It is almost too much," she said out loud.

Bidzel had moved farther down and was now

studying another line. He turned to Kurak'Kahn. "Overseer, there is a lot of information here. As you can tell, Yuma'qia and I are overwhelmed with this discovery. May we take some time to study it further before making any more declarations? We do not wish to be in error. As I said, it will take years to understand, but I believe we can give you a fair overview if we can have a few days."

"Of course. We are in no hurry to leave. There is nothing of more importance than this," said Kurak'Kahn.

"You are welcome to stay as long as you wish," agreed Khon'Tor. He had an idea but would only share it after talking with Haan.

Khon'Tor signaled for the Sarnonn to come with him. The two walked out of the chamber and a way down the hall.

"Haan, I have discussed this with my Circle of Counsel, Acaraho, Adia, Awan, and some others. We all agree. We would like to turn Kthama Minor over to you and your followers—with your permission for us to enter and investigate the history further."

"You want us to live here? You are saying that we can live here? At Kthama Minor?"

"Yes. I decided this before I knew we were related. You have helped us immensely, and it is because of us that you and your followers are homeless. We will be glad to get you set up—bedding, water baskets, food, whatever you need."

Haan blinked. "This is unspeakably generous,

Khon'Tor. My people will be very grateful, as am I. Does Haaka know?"

"No. The offer is yours to accept or not."

Haan thought of how happy Haaka would be. He knew she loved life at Kthama. Despite his attempts to control himself because of Hakani's death being so recent, Haan was finally admitting to himself that he cared for Haaka.

"This is a new start for the Sassen, and your offer of help is also very generous. But I would like to ask for more than physical provisions. I have seen, and so has Haaka, how organized your people are, how everyone works together for the better good of all. We have much to learn from you, and the workings of your community are some of them."

"We will be glad to help you with that. I will speak with the others and see who would be best to guide you in organizing your new culture."

The Sarnonn Leader extended his hands, palms up, and Khon'Tor, catching the cue, slid his palms over Haan's in the Sassen statement of brotherhood.

"Perhaps we should leave the record keepers to themselves. After you are set up in here, do you mind if they move into one of the living quarters, so they are closer? That is if they wish to," he added, realizing that living among the Sarnonn might prove to be too much for their nerves. There were some base survival reactions that even reason could not overrule.

Haan being happy with that request, they returned to the others.

"I suggest that we leave the record keepers to their task for the moment. I have offered Kthama Minor to Haan and his people, and he has accepted. I have also offered our help with initial provisions and setting up systems. I doubt any of our sleeping mats would suffice for them, but we can show them where our materials come from and help them get started," Khon'Tor announced.

He turned to Haan, "How many of your group are females?"

"Of the forty, about a third."

"Is there any chance that any of the others still at Kayerm would join you if they could?"

"I do not know. But I would not wish to entice them with a promise of life at Kthama Minor. In fact, it is best if they do not know. Contact between us is not something I would advise. I believe we are past the point of no return in the rift between my people, and it would probably take Straf'Tor himself to change their minds."

"We can discuss future steps at a different time. Perhaps there is another band of Sarnonn that you could recruit. We stand at the beginning of an era of cooperation between our two peoples; perhaps another community would also be willing to work together with us."

Haan nodded, anxious to tell Haaka. "When may I bring my people down here?"

"If you could give them a while to examine the chamber further, I think that would go well for their nerves. They are not yet used to your size and presence."

"That is fair. I would like to tell Haaka, though—and I have not seen her or Kalli for some time."

"Of course. I will collect my people and return to Kthama too."

Acaraho had one of the guards lead Haan to Haaka's quarters. She barely left the cave system, content to live inside the convenience and luxury Kthama provided. When Haan arrived, she was sitting on the floor playing with Kalli.

Haaka rose to her feet and rushed to Haan. Forgetting herself, she hugged him. "Oh. I am so glad to see you. Have you come to stay with me finally?" she asked, forgetting herself all over again.

"No, but I have come with just as good news," he said.

"What? What is it?" she was almost giddy with excitement.

"Khon'Tor has given us Kthama Minor. It is ours if we want it. We can move there in a few days. They said they would help us model our community after theirs, teach us how to be organized as they are—

work together as one. They also offered baskets and other provisions," Haan chuckled, imagining one of the Akassa's smaller tools in their large Sassen hands.

"I am so happy to hear this, Haan. You know I did not want to leave Kthama. After this, returning to Kayerm would be hard—even if it were a choice, which I know it is not."

Haan looked at Haaka. She was smiling broadly, and he realized her happiness made him happy too. He decided to wait no longer.

"I know it has not been very long since Hakani's death, and you are part of my pod, so I hope you do not think it wrong of me. I would not ask if Hakani were still alive, as it would be her right to select a second female on my behalf, but she is gone now, and our separation has made me realize that I care for you. If you are willing, I ask you to be my mate."

Haaka froze. She could not believe her ears. "Haan," she stammered. "I have always looked up to you. But without Hakani's permission, I would never have told you how I felt."

He pulled her close and hugged her. Kalli cooed and gurgled from the floor.

"I will not rush you, Haaka. When you are ready, we will make the bond. And then, only when you are ready to receive me, will we mate."

He is as kind as I have always known him to be. Dear Hakani, I believe you would bless this union. It was you who encouraged me to take care of Kalli should anything happen to you. I wonder if you had plans at that time to take your own life, or if you were just speaking out of conjecture. No one knows what life will bring, and I never imagined I would be Haan's mate.

Haaka was excited to share the news. "May I go and tell the other females?" she asked.

Haan thought for a moment. "I need to tell the others that we will be moving into Kthama Minor; it will bring them great relief. I would like Khon'Tor to come with us, perhaps some of the others. Let me make those arrangements, and I will come back for you," he said.

A guard was stationed outside the room in case Haaka needed anything, and Haan asked him where Khon'Tor might be found. The guard accompanied him to the Great Chamber to look for First Guard Awan, who was sometimes there with the High Protector during working hours. One of them would know Khon'Tor's whereabouts.

As Haan entered, Awan was telling Acaraho about Khon'Tor's request for a sparring partner.

Acaraho turned to Haan. "Adik'Tar, how may I help you?" he asked.

"I would like you, Khon'Tor, and whomever else Khon'Tor chooses to come with me, to tell my people that we will be moving into Kthama Minor at some point. I would like them to hear about this gift from the Akassa Adik'Tar himself. Haaka and I are to be paired, so I would also like her to come with us to share the news."

"Congratulations. Very well. We have time now, before the next meeting, if you like. I will take you to Khon'Tor now."

Before long, Khon'Tor and almost his entire Circle of Counsel was ready to hike up the path to the meadow above Kthama. Nadiwani was watching Kalli for Haaka.

They set out, and Adia immediately noticed the same profuse growth along the way. Not being able to hold back any longer, she said, "How are you not all noticing the early changes in the vegetation? Several feet on both sides, ahead and behind us." The others stopped to look. In the turmoil, they had not particularly taken in their surroundings.

"It is the same growth we saw along the path to the Healer's Cove," said Urilla Wuti.

As they breached the crest to the meadow, each of them stopped their forward movement in awe of what they were seeing, finally understanding what Adia had been trying to point out.

The grass throughout the meadow was green and lush. Wildflowers were already pushing up through the ground. Along the perimeters, fruit trees were in blossom. Birds hopped about in search of insects as they emerged from the warm soil. A deer with two fawns stepped out from the treeline. Several rabbits hopped across the open expanse, and squirrels chattered from the trees.

The scent of spring was in the air, even though spring should be weeks away from coming to the land.

Then Adia saw the circle of giant rocks that had been embedded into the ground and gasped. What had recently been twelve slabs of grey granite were now sparkling, clear crystal. She had never seen anything like it.

The others followed her gaze and stood there in awe, mesmerized by the shining monoliths.

"What is going on?" Adia said. "Haan, what has happened here? I first noticed the plants growing on the path between the Great Entrance and the Healer's Cove. And now here. And look at the rocks you placed!"

"To open Kthama Minor," explained Haan, "we had collectively to channel the power of the Great Spirit. In making that connection, we opened a concentrated flow of the Aezaitera into Etera. The loving creative force, the life force—that which moves within all we see and know—enlivens everything around us. The influx of spirit emanated from us as we moved along."

As he spoke, Haan realized why the first preparation area had been destroyed. *If we had stayed in the first place, our march here would have led Tarnor and his rebels directly to Kthama. If nothing else, they would only have had to follow the trail of the early-blooming vegeta-*

tion. But that does not answer the question of who destroyed it, only perhaps why. He made a note to talk to Artadel when the excitement of his announcement about Kthama Minor had died down.

As Artadel and some of the males approached, Haaka ran over to greet the females. They had many questions about Kalli and life at Kthama, and Haaka did not say anything about pairing with Haan. She would wait for him to make that announcement, as well as to explain the generous invitation to move into Kthama Minor.

Haan addressed the group once they were quiet.

"My Sassen family," Haan began. "Thanks to you, Kthama Minor is open and sharing her secrets—secrets that have been hidden for generations. Secrets which will hopefully provide answers for both Sassen and Akassa. It has been an uncertain journey, and I thank you each for staying with me and supporting the vision of brotherhood between the Sassen and the Akassa. As far as Rah-hora is concerned, I do not have any answers. I do not believe it is a threat to us any longer. I am not sure now if it ever was. Perhaps its only power was our belief in it—but there is time to think about that later. What we have come to tell you is that the Akassa have offered Kthama Minor to us. I do not need to explain to you how generous this gift is."

The crowd nodded and murmured in excitement. Several male and female pairs embraced each other.

Khon'Tor could tell that this was great news for

them and reflected on how close he had come to being homeless for his crimes against Adia, only even worse—banished from Kthama and all the People to live in exile, alone, forever.

He stood forward to speak. "You are welcome here. We have some work to do in understanding the Wall of Records and ask your forbearance as that may take some time. We will need permanent access to that area but will be discreet. If any of our supplies will help you, you are welcome to them. We all look forward to a partnership between the Sassen and the Akassa."

Adia was listening but could not help being distracted by the transformation around her. Though nowhere near as vibrant and alive, the surroundings reminded her a tiny bit of the Corridor. A ladybug landed on her, and she watched it crawl up her arm.

Whatever they did, they opened some path that brought the Great Mother's life force here in high concentration, thought Adia. *It makes sense that they would need more than their own power to open Kthama Minor. Whatever ritual they performed to join as one mind and one body also joined them even more deeply with the Great Spirit. And everywhere they walked, the power leaked out—for lack of a better phrase. That is why the path between here and the Healer's Cove is bursting with early spring. And even more so, the meadow here, where they have spent so much time.*

Haan continued, "I have much more to share, but now that our needs for a home have been met, there is time for that. I will let you know when we may move in. In the meantime, I have other news."

He paused a moment, "I know it has not been that long since my mate, Hakani, took her own life. We have also recently been through much turmoil, and some would say that life-changing decisions should not be made during times of stress. However, this decision is one that will provide great support for me, as your Leader, especially now, when there are only more and bigger changes to come." He paused and put a hand out to Haaka, who stepped closer. "So, I ask for your blessing as I share with you that I will be taking Haaka as my own."

Heads nodded everywhere. They had accepted Hakani, and many of them had even grieved her death with Haan. But at the same time, they were glad that Haan was taking another mate; the current of life must keep moving forward.

Haaka was speculating to herself that perhaps before too long, Kalli would have a playmate.

While Khon'Tor and Haan were speaking to the crowd, Acaraho was taking everything in. He was studying the twelve giant, crystallized stones. And had one not moved, he might never have seen them. Lined up, one in front of each of the giant crystals, were twelve giant Sarnonn, each covered in silver-white hair. In front of the crystals, they were nearly invisible. Acaraho had seen the Sarnonn before when they first came up to the meadow, but he had not noticed any of them with that coloring. He turned to Adia, "Where did the silver-haired ones come from? I know they were not here originally. I would never have missed that; it is too striking. It reminds me of the coloring of Moc'Tor."

"You are right," said Adia, her voice low. "They were not in the original group, and there is the same number of them as the rocks that have turned to crystal. Yet, overall, the numbers seem the same—" her voice trailed off.

After a while, Khon'Tor and the others left the Sarnonn to their celebration and discussion. He knew that Haan and Haaka would be inundated with questions because none of the others had been inside either Kthama or Kthama Minor.

CHAPTER 12

Oh'Dar was becoming anxious to get back to the village and Acise. With everything going on around the High Council's visit, he thought it might be an appropriate time to return. That evening, he broached with his parents the subject of returning to the Brothers.

"I think the High Council will be here for some time, son. Your mother and I are fine with your leaving for a while. Perhaps you can make plans for your pairing with Acise and when you return you can tell us when it will take place. We would both like to be there if it will not be too disruptive," Acaraho said.

"It would create interest," said Oh'Dar diplomatically, "but I think it would be good. It will bring the People and the Brothers closer. Even more so now that our tribes are being joined through my pairing with Acise."

Adia noted with pleasure that Oh'Dar, not really aware of what he had just said, subconsciously identified himself as one of the People.

"With the Chief's passing, I think this would be a good thing, Oh'Dar," agreed Adia.

"I will take Storm and leave this morning. Is there anything you want me to bring back?"

"I believe Khon'Tor mentioned that the Overseer would like you to make a necklace for his mate, similar to the one you made for Tehya. And I am sure Khon'Tor would appreciate a second design, as a surprise for her," Adia said.

"I will bring back as many stones as I can carry. Which reminds me that I must take the saddlebags."

"We are very happy for you, Oh'Dar. When this settles down, we look forward to your bringing Acise here—" she stopped. *Where will they live? Her parents are there, but we are here—and when our males are paired, we are used to the females coming to live here.* "—Of course, where you choose to live is up to you, but I hope you will also spend time here with us."

Oh'Dar got up to hug her. "I could never stay away from you for long, Mama. I will have to return to Shadow Ridge someday, and will probably take Acise with me, but I will not stay away again as long as I did, I promise."

Adia picked up his hand and kissed it, then patted him. "Off with you. Ride carefully."

Oh'Dar arrived at the Brothers' village to find a hubbub of activity. He rode Storm over to see what all the fuss was about. As he pulled the horse around, Is'Taqa came over to greet him.

Oh'Dar dismounted and put his hand on Is'Taqa's shoulder. "What is going on here? It looks like some big project."

Out of the crowd came a flurry of buckskin skirts and Acise launched herself into his arms. He caught her up readily, and she wrapped her arms around his neck.

"Oh, you are back! Come see, you must come and see!" and she dragged Oh'Dar through the crowd. He looked back at Is'Taqa as she took his hand and led him away.

The crowd, which turned out to be a work crew, parted to make way for them. In front of Oh'Dar was a new structure going up. It was situated in a beautiful part of their land, near the tree line. The entrance faced east to catch the morning sun, and the rest of it was protected from the elements by a hillside, the direction from which most bad weather came in.

"What is this?" he asked.

"It is our new shelter. They are building one just for us. But see, it is not that far from my parents. I am so excited," she exclaimed.

"I can see that," he chuckled, happy to see her like this. "It is very pleasing. I will have to thank everyone, but what can I provide in return?" he asked.

"Just give us many healthy grandchildren, Oh'Dar," said a voice behind him, and he turned to see Honovi smiling at them both.

"I will do my best," Oh'Dar smiled, a vision running through his imagination of a little Acise with blue eyes.

"We always expected that our children and their partners would live with us in our shelter. But it somehow seemed right for you two to have your own place," Honovi explained as Is'Taqa joined her. "It is more in keeping with the People's ways, and it is not fair that you should make all the adjustments."

One by one, the others came and greeted him. Oh'Dar's heart was warmed by the show of support. Unsurprisingly, Pajackok was absent. His father was present, however, and came over.

"Oh'Dar, welcome back," said Tac'agawa.

"Thank you. I am so sorry for the loss of Chief Ogima Adoeete. It is also a great loss for the People," he said.

Tac'agawa nodded, then paused. "I am aware of Pajackok's behavior. For this, I apologize. I hope in time the sting will pass."

"I can understand how he feels, Tac'agawa. We were friends growing up, and I hope we can find our way back to that again."

Tac'agawa nodded and turned to rejoin the crew.

"Now that you are back, can we plan our bonding ceremony?" Acise asked.

"If Chief Is'Taqa thinks enough time has passed for it to be respectful, yes," Oh'Dar answered, nodding to the new Chief and finding it peculiar to speak of Is'Taqa so formally.

"We have been talking, and we were thinking of the next new moon."

"A time of new beginnings."

"Yes. And the shelter will be done by then."

"My parents would like to attend if it would not cause too much of a disturbance," said Oh'Dar.

"We would be pleased to have them here. It would be an honor," Is'Taqa replied.

"How long are you staying? I want to show you the inside once the others are done," said Acise.

"I will stay for several days. I need to visit the stream and the lower caves. Khon'Tor would like another necklace for Tehya."

"I do not mind helping you look," exclaimed Acise, "and maybe Snana would also like to come. I know Noshoba would enjoy it too."

Oh'Dar smiled, remembering times in the past when they would sit with him as little girls and show him all their collection of treasures, many of which he had found for them. He would pick up each one they gave him and turn it over, talking about what its best use might be, helping them plan their projects.

"Let me put Storm up; I will be back in a few moments."

"Before you go——" Acise stood up on her tiptoes and gave Oh'Dar a tender kiss, and he resisted the impulse to kiss her deep and hard. *The next month is going to feel like forever—but it does give me time to ask about the Ashwea Tare. I do hope she does not expect me to be good at it right away.*

They spent the afternoon helping to find more materials for their shelter. Acise showed him the new buckskin she was sewing for the ceremony. Oh'Dar was content, grateful that he and not Pajackok would be standing next to her.

Bidzel and Yuma'qia had been diligently studying the Wall of Records. Haan and his people had brought in boulders for them to climb to reach the markings that were higher up. They quit only long enough to eat and to get the most meager amount of sleep. They were anxious to share with Khon'Tor and the High Council what they had learned, but they first had to be very sure about what they were seeing.

They finally sent word that they were ready.

Khon'Tor, his Circle of Counsel, and the High Council members stood at the entrance to the Wall of Records. Haan and Haaka stood behind, well able to see over the heads of those gathered in front of them.

"We cannot tell you what a find of this historical

significance represents," said Bidzel. "Just the little Yuma'qia and I have learned over the past few days has drastically changed our understanding of the past. So much of what we believed has been in error. Whether intentionally distorted or just lost through the passing on of stories, we will never know. We will show you the highlights now and the more subtle differences later. Come."

Bidzel led them inside and pointed to just inside the interior left wall. "It starts here with the rule of Moc'Tor. There are no earlier records, but perhaps there was no need—or no foresight about how important records would become. At that time, the females lived here in Kthama Minor with their offspring. The males lived at Kthama, which they called Kthama Prime. But even with the division, their numbers were crushing. They were looking at having to severely curtail their population growth but were not sure how. Moc'Tor issued an order that the males could no longer mate at will and that the females must choose one male with whom they would mate exclusively. It created a great deal of strife, as you can imagine, with a shift in power from the males to the females.

"There was also a great sickness. The Mothoc believed it was a punishment from the Great Spirit for their indiscriminate mating. Once the sickness passed, it was decided to interbreed with those whom we know as the Brothers. They are represented here by the Brothers' mark. This is what created the great division."

"How do you know that?" asked Kurak'Kahn.

"Because of how the pairings continued, Overseer. Moc'Tor's line here, continued breeding with the Brothers far past where this other line stopped— this other line being that of Moc'Tor's brother, Straf'-Tor. It is also the faction that left Kthama for Kayerm —the Sarnonn, as Haan explained. But the lines of division were not perfectly split. Some of Straf'Tor's line also continued with Moc'Tor's way of thinking. The descendants of Moc'Tor's group mostly stayed here and became us—the People—but some left for other communities, just as did some of Straf'Tor's followers."

"Haan, here is your line," and Yuma'qia pointed to a series of marks that branched off from Straf'-Tor's. "Here is the mark for the Brothers," he said, pointing to another, "which is also the Sarnonn's mark for the Others."

They stood there for a while, studying the markings, trying to see what Bidzel and Yuma'qia were pointing out. Khon'Tor could clearly see the 'Tor mark as it continued from Moc'Tor and what must have been the mark of E'ranale, his mate, through several other branches.

"It looks like Moc'Tor had several offspring."

"Yes, this one here was his daughter Pan. And you can see here—and here—where the symbols for the Brothers start to drop off. This, here, is the point at which it looks like the pairings produced true, meaning they no longer had to introduce the Brothers' bloodline. People could mate with the People and produce offspring looking just like them. Of course, the varying times at which the Brothers' influence stopped account for the differences between us in hair coloring, height, build, and so on throughout our communities."

Harak'Sar stepped forward. "Where is my line?" he asked. Bidzel and Yuma'qia quickly glanced at each other.

Yuma'qia cleared his throat. "This is one of the more interesting finds," and he stepped across the room, the others following him.

'This is the line of Tres'Sar, your ancestor. This is the line of the People of the Far High Hills," said Yuma'qia.

Harak'Sar, Urilla Wuti, and Tehya gathered close; this was the history of their community.

They studied the markings for a while. Then Tehya noticed something that was not in the others.

"Bidzel, please. What is that mark there? I see the marks for the Brothers—"

Bidzel looked at Khon'Tor and the Overseer, then at Harak'Sar before answering Tehya.

"That is the mark symbolizing, as best we can tell, *the white ones from the icy waters.*"

Everyone turned to look at Tehya. Then back at Bidzel, then at each other.

"I do not understand," said Harak'Sar, very sure

that he did, however. "The Mothoc bred with the Waschini?"

"From what I can see at the moment, mostly only in these lines here." Bidzel motioned to several places on the wall under Harak'Sar's line. "It may have been proximity or chance. But there is Waschini blood entering in many places," and he pointed to the marks as he called them out.

Haan stepped forward, "Yes. Straf'Tor and Tres'Sar were at great odds over this. It caused a huge uproar. Straf'Tor was very angry. Where it entered, greater changes showed up than in the offling from the Others' seed. Very much lighter coloring, much less hair, very, very small. The Waschini blood has a strong influence; where it appears, it overpowers Mothoc traits far more quickly than does the Brothers'."

"But that is my family mark next to the Waschini's—" started Tehya, and then her voice trailed off as every head turned in her direction. Tehya could practically feel eyes upon her, looking her up and down. Her delicate feet, the light nails, the nearly hairless legs, on up to her lower wrappings, under which they could imagine that she had no natural thick covering for modesty. Her pale skin up over her belly, her comparatively delicate bone structure. And then the almost golden hair and the amber eyes. Now that they stopped and looked, nearly everything about her indicated Waschini influence. How could they all have missed it?

Khon'Tor was overcome with his own thoughts.

Tehya. My beloved Tehya has Waschini blood in her. It is so apparent now. How delicate her features are. How pink her lips—

Crumbling under their scrutiny and filled with shame, Tehya stumbled backward. Khon'Tor was immediately at her side, encasing her in his embrace. Adia and Urilla Wuti quickly stepped over to them.

"No, no, no," said Adia. "Do not be upset, Tehya. By the Mother, why are you upset?" She stroked Tehya's hair.

"I am Waschini, I am of the White Wasters," and she buried her face in her hands.

Khon'Tor used his will to pull himself together, but inside, his heart was breaking. *It is my fault; I am the one who has spoken out the loudest about the Waschini. And yet nothing has come of the invasion we pictured and Oh'Dar is one of our greatest blessings.* "Tehya. Look at me. If you want a label, I will give you one. You are Spirit-sent. You are the perfect mate to me, and I would not change a thing about you. You are *beautiful*. What does it matter if Waschini blood runs in your veins? Look at Oh'Dar. He is Waschini, and he has done nothing but bless our people and improve the lives of us all. Our daughter, precious Arismae, would not be here without his help, and most likely, you would not, either.

"If we want to talk about grievous acts, we have only to look at our history for that—taking the Brothers without their consent. Civil war and division among our ancestors. I will not have you thinking badly of yourself because of that," he said, pointing back to the marks on the wall.

She clutched his chest hair with her fingers and buried her face against him, swallowing her tears.

"This is enough of a history lesson for today," and Khon'Tor swept her up and carried her out.

The others stood a while, talking among themselves. Only Adia and Acaraho followed Khon'Tor and Tehya outside.

Partway down the path, they felt the ground shake and turned to see Haan sprinting to catch up. The running Sarnonn was an imposing sight, and Adia instinctively stepped behind Acaraho.

Haan came to an abrupt stop and stooped down to talk to Tehya, who was still in Khon'Tor's arms.

"Little one, mate of Khon'Tor, you misunderstand. The Mothoc did not stop breeding with the Waschini because the Waschini are bad. They stopped breeding because the Waschini blood was too strong. It overpowered the Mothoc blood. Change is hard for our people. A little change could be accepted, but the offling of the Waschini seed were too different. Clever, fast, just like Others—but for some unknown reason, too little Mothoc influence remained. The Mothoc blood *must not disappear from Etera.*"

Khon'Tor motioned for Acaraho and Adia to follow him and carried Tehya back to the Leader's

Quarters. He stopped on the way and asked someone to have Mapiya bring Arismae to them. Seating Tehya safely on the big, overstuffed chair, he knelt in front of her. Acaraho was standing behind, while Adia looked through the food stores for something to calm Tehya and help her rest.

Khon'Tor placed his hands on his mate's knees and looked at her. She had stopped crying, but her face was still tear-stained, and her eyes red. He brushed the hair away from her forehead.

Adia brought something in a little gourd bowl for Tehya to drink.

Tehya rubbed her eyes, took it and sipped, while Khon'Tor continued to stare intently at her.

Then Mapiya entered with Arismae.

Tehya set down the little bowl and reached for the precious bundle. She took her tiny offspring in her arms and cuddled her. "Now I know why her eyes are so light. Lighter than yours or mine when ordinarily that would never be. And why she is so small. Haan said the Waschini blood overpowers ours," she whispered to Khon'Tor.

Khon'Tor stood up and stroked the top of her head. He signaled to the others to join him outside in the tunnel so Tehya could nurse their offspring in private.

Once outside, shaking his head, he said to Acaraho and Adia, "Now I am trying to remember all the times I might have spoken against the Waschini."

"None of us saw it, Khon'Tor. But now that we know, I do not see how we could *not* have seen it; in retrospect, it is so obvious," said Adia.

"At home, there are several families in which smaller stature and lighter coloring run. But if anyone knew of this, it was never mentioned to me," said Urilla Wuti. She expected that, as a Healer, she would have known about history such as this.

"Prejudice is a terrible thing, I see that now," said Khon'Tor. "I was wrong about Oh'Dar, as I have been wrong about other things."

"It is just a shock. To learn something about yourself which you never knew," offered Adia. "I wish Oh'Dar were still here; perhaps he could help her."

Acaraho was quiet, deep in thought.

Khon'Tor turned to Adia, "I have matters to attend to tomorrow. Do you think you could arrange for someone to stay here with Tehya? I do not want her alone with her thoughts. I will check in as much as I can during the day."

"I will take care of it. I promise," answered Adia.

After Khon'Tor had left Kthama Minor with Tehya and the others, the High Council members also adjourned at the suggestion of Bidzel and Yuma'qia. The record keepers were not ready to reveal any more of what they had discovered until the others had adjusted to the revelations of that day.

The next morning, First Guard Awan found Khon'Tor with Acaraho. "Good news, Adoeete. I have found you a sparring partner."

"Good." Khon'Tor shot a look at Acaraho, realizing that the High Protector knew about his request. "Tell him to meet me in the Great Entrance tonight at twilight. Right now, I am going back to check on Tehya," and Khon'Tor rose from the table where they had been sitting. *Good. I need this. I have to find proof that Akar is dead. Or find him and dispatch him myself. The nightmares continue to haunt Tehya, and I know what is causing them. It is my presence because Akar and I are almost identical. He held her captive for several days. No doubt, my being there at night is triggering her nightmares about him. Until she knows he is dead, until I can bring her proof, she will live in fear of him forever.*

That evening, Khon'Tor entered the Great Chamber. Two staffs cut from flexible green wood were leaning against the rock wall. Ahead of him stood a male, only his back visible.

"Thank you for agreeing to this. I do not mean to harm you. But I need you to test me."

The figure turned around to face Khon'Tor.

"I will do my best," said Acaraho.

"*You?*" said Khon'Tor.

"You asked for someone your size. That does not leave much choice."

"I also asked for someone younger."

Acaraho smiled and raised his hands, palms out. "This is the closest it is going to get, Adik'Tar."

"Very well, then. No doubt we will both end up bruised."

"I know why you are doing this," said Acaraho. "I could come with you."

"I do not need help."

"You would better leave that decision until you see how you feel when we are done."

Khon'Tor laughed, the first light-heartedness he had felt in weeks.

He walked over and picked up one of the practice staffs, the one which most resembled a pliable young seedling. It would not do any great harm but would sting and perhaps leave a welt.

"For Adia's sake, I hate to mark your body."

"I would hate to have it marked. Adia likes it the way it is," Acaraho answered, whipping his staff through the air to test it.

Khon'Tor circled him. Without warning, Acaraho lashed out and landed a wicked strike against Khon'Tor.

"That was not within the rules of conduct," he snarled, wincing in pain.

"Oh, I am sorry? Do you expect Akar will be following the rules of conduct?"

"Good point," said the Leader as he lashed out in return.

Acaraho dodged the end of Khon'Tor's staff, but only barely. He heard it whisk over his arm and felt it brush his body hair. He lunged at Khon'Tor, who blocked him with the pole, spinning around and catching Acaraho's back on the return. Acaraho gasped and ducked just in time to miss the back-swing. Crouched down, he tackled Khon'Tor behind the knees, knocking the Leader to the ground.

Khon'Tor's staff rolled away out of his reach. He scrambled to retrieve it just as Acaraho kicked him over onto his back and pressed a foot on his chest, pretending to drive his staff through Khon'Tor's mid-section.

"*Rok*," swore Khon'Tor. "That did not take long."

"It has been a long time since either of us was in hand-to-hand combat. But remember you did fight Akar'Tor. I was there. He was no match for you in any way."

"I cannot assume that he has not received instruction somewhere since then. He is still younger; his reflexes are faster. He may well have more stamina."

"That is true, he *is* younger and his reflexes faster, and when you fought him the first time, he thought that would be enough. As you did before, you must defeat him in a way that does not depend on speed. It does not matter how you defeat him, Khon'Tor. It must just be done. But unless he has gained skills and technique, he will not want to fight you one-on-one. He learned that the last time."

"I did not think you would best me."

Acaraho smiled. "I did," and he patted Khon'Tor on the shoulder as he went to put up his staff.

One step away, Acaraho turned back and swung his weapon around just in time to block Khon'Tor's sneak attack, the impact breaking Khon'Tor's staff in two. It flew from his hands and rolled across the rock floor in pieces.

"*That* is what I am talking about. Good thinking," said Acaraho.

"How did you know I was going to do that?" asked Khon'Tor. "I thought I had you."

"Because that is what I would have done. But, Khon'Tor, there is one fatal flaw you cannot afford to ignore. And if you do not face it, it will get you killed instead of Akar'Tor."

"What is that?"

"The fact that part of you does not want to kill your son."

He is right. I do not. I do, but I do not. I hope to find him dead already. I do not want to kill anyone's son, but I do want to kill the PetaQ who kidnapped Tehya and terrorized her. And Acaraho is right—at the crucial moment, that hesitation might be all Akar needs to kill me first.

"Until you make peace with this—until you remove every trace of reluctance or second thought—it is not safe for you to face him. He will have no such feelings of guilt about killing you."

"Thank you, Acaraho. I know what I need to do—"

"You need to talk to Haan," said Acaraho, finishing the thought for him.

Khon'Tor picked up some food on his way to join Tehya in their quarters. She was not there, so he left to find her, passing Mapiya and Pakuna in one of the tunnels.

"Have you seen my mate?" he stopped and asked the females.

"Yes. We spent the day with her and Adia and Nadiwani in Oh'Dar's workshop. She wanted to make something for Arismae. She might still be there; we just left them."

Khon'Tor thanked the females and continued. As he walked, he thought, *Acaraho must truly have forgiven me for what I did to Adia. There is no way we could have sparred if he had not; he would not have passed up the chance to inflict great harm, if not kill me. He told me that he was my ally when Akar first took Tehya, and I do now believe it is true.*

Khon'Tor poked his head into the workshop. "Anyone still here?" he asked.

"Come on in. We are just finishing up," said Nadiwani.

"Show him what you made, Tehya, go ahead," said Nimida.

Tehya held up a tiny little wrapping, dyed with pastel colors, and with little embellishments.

Khon'Tor could not help but laugh out loud. "That is adorable. Seriously?" He smiled again, then walked over and took it from her hands and held it up in front of him, turning it around.

"I cannot wait to see her in it. I am thinking of calling a general assembly; please make sure she has it on. I think you may start a trend. He returned it to Tehya. "I fetched food. Are you ready to go home?"

She nodded, piled her creations into his arms, and picked up Arismae. She adjusted her daughter safely in the sling and prepared to leave.

"Tomorrow?" she asked, and the other females smiled and nodded.

Khon'Tor took her hand as they headed to their quarters. "It sounds as if you had a good day." He smiled down at her as they walked.

"I did; I enjoy having friends, and we had a lot of fun. Why are you calling a meeting?"

"It is more of a celebration really, but it will have to wait until Oh'Dar returns. I would like to announce his pairing with Is'Taqa's daughter. And I would like Is'Taqa and his family also to attend if possible. I think we have enough in the stores to make it festive."

"It sounds like fun, a nice change. It seems as if lately, most of our assemblies have been serious."

Khon'Tor realized she was right. He wondered if perhaps Acaraho and Adia might also want to announce that Adia was with offspring.

"That is an excellent point, Saraste'," he remarked. "I think we should meet and think of every good thing that has happened recently and make a point of mentioning them all. We have some new offspring in the community; maybe the parents would like to stand up and be acknowledged."

"I can mention it to my friends tomorrow. They might also have some ideas."

"Wait," she said suddenly. They stopped.

"The High Council is here. If they are still here when Oh'Dar and Acise are to be paired, could not the Overseer pronounce Ashwea Awhidi over them?" she asked.

"Now that would be a good focus for the celebration. And then we can add to it with all the other good news." Khon'Tor again thought to himself how smart she was.

"If you want, I can ask Adia about it tomorrow. I am sure the High Council will be here for some time."

No doubt, thought Khon'Tor. *I do not see the work on the Wall of Records ending anytime soon, though, at some point, the other Leaders will have to return to their communities. But Bidzel, Yuma'qia, and maybe the Overseer will stay. No one will be able to drag the record keepers away for some time.*

Everyone was thrilled with Khon'Tor's idea of a celebration, and Adia was especially pleased with the
idea of Oh'Dar and Acise being paired in a special
Ashwea Awhidi. She asked Acaraho what he
thought, and he agreed with it all, including
announcing that she was with offspring. With spring
and rebirth coming to Etera, it was perfect timing.

Having something to look forward to, spirits
picked up, and the mysterious fact of Kthama Minor
and all its secrets faded to the background for a little
while.

Khon'Tor made the trek up the meadow to find
Haan. All the fruit trees along the perimeter were
now in full bloom. Bees were busy pollinating every
flower and blossom in sight. The rest of Etera was
still largely dormant, but here, spring was in full
force.

Haan stood with Artadel, pointing into a stand of
trees and discussing something. They heard
Khon'Tor approach and turned to greet him.

He looked around. "Where is everyone?"

"They are out gathering materials for Kthama
Minor. There is much work to be done before we can
move in."

Khon'Tor nodded.

"What is on your mind, Adik'Tar?" Haan asked
him, seeing the burden he carried in his features.

"Haan," began Khon'Tor, and he exhaled.

"I will speak with you later, Artadel," said Haan, dismissing his Healer.

"Is it your little Tehya? Is she still upset over being part Waschini?" he asked.

"It is partly that, but more. She has nightmares. Every night. Every night since we rescued her from Akar. Nothing I can do stops them. She is not getting enough rest, and it is wearing her down."

Haan understood. "We do not know if Akar'Tor is still alive. It would be best to know one way or the other."

Khon'Tor nodded. "It is worse than that. I think I remind her of him. She wakes up in terror, thinking he is in the room, but it is me."

Haan pursed his lips. "Are you going to look for him?"

"Yes."

"And if you find him?"

Silence. Khon'Tor ran his hand through the silver streak in his hair.

"Are you asking *my* permission to kill your son?" asked Haan.

"No. Akar'Tor is my son by blood only. I am asking permission to kill *yours*."

Haan turned and looked up at the sky. He closed his eyes and stood silent for a moment. Khon'Tor waited.

"I cannot give you permission to kill Akar'Tor. But I will tell you that the monster who kidnapped Tehya is not who I raised. I did not recognize him.

Perhaps it is something from his mother's blood, but in that twisted mind, I saw no part of the offling I raised. He turned on his mother, attacked her, and threatened to kill her for not helping him recapture Tehya."

"Of course, Haan. It is my burden, my sin to bear, not yours."

"I will tell you though," Haan looked back down at Khon'Tor, his eyes steady and his voice low, "if anyone had done to my mate as was done to yours, and his existence caused a continued threat to her welfare and that of her offling, I would feel the same as you. And I would not rest until the matter was settled."

It is the closest he can come to saying he will not condemn me. Khon'Tor nodded, then changed the subject. "Have you decided when you and Haaka will be paired?"

"When we officially move into Kthama Minor. However, it is a name filled with much burdensome history, and this is a time of new beginnings for my people. I would like to rename it," Haan said.

"It is yours now, and I think that is a good idea. A new chapter."

Khon'Tor slowly trudged back to Kthama, a great deal on his mind.

The night fire outside Kayerm was dying down. Dorn and Tarnor crouched before it, waiting for the last embers to burn. Overhead, the stars in the dark sky were only partly diminished by a few clouds. A coyote howled in the far distance, the only sound now that the crackling of the flames had ceased.

A branch snapped, and both Dorn and Tarnor jumped to their feet and spun around.

"What are *you* doing here?" asked Tarnor.

PLEASE READ

Dear Readers,

Welcome back. Here we are at the end of Book Eight. I am grateful that you find the series interesting enough to stay with it. It is validation for me that I was not out of my mind to write these stories, and it pleases me that you are getting enjoyment out of reading them.

If you know of others who might enjoy the series, please tell them about it. I have two more series planned in this line. Continued sales are what fund the books to come.

The next book is Book Nine: Retribution. If you would like to be notified when the next book in this series is available, you can join the mailing list by visiting my website at:

https://leighrobertsauthor.com/contact

You are also welcome to join me on FB at The Etera Chronicles.

Thank you.

—Leigh

ACKNOWLEDGMENTS

I want to acknowledge my own Circle of Council; my husband, my brother Richard, my brother-in-law Tim, my editor Joy and my cover designer Cherie (who along the way have turned into beloved friends), my fellow authors. There are others I no doubt should mention but I want to specifically shout out to my dear friends Carolene and Marsha who have steadfastly stood by me, cheering me on through all of this.

The definition of friends has changed as the reach across the world through the power of the internet has drawn us closer than ever before. To me, fiction authors are like scientists—above the separating forces of politics, religion—bound instead at the soul level by a common dedication.

Since becoming an author, my list encompasses friends from around the globe. My editor is in South Africa; my cover designer in the UK; loved ones in the USA; and my fellow authors are scattered even to Australia and New Zealand.

So to all of you, near or far; thank you for your friendship, your support, and for sharing this journey with me.

They say if you have three good friend you can consider yourself blessed. So on that basis—I am blessed, *indeed*.

Made in the USA
Las Vegas, NV
09 February 2024

85513259R00173